I WON'T LET YOU GO

COLE BAXTER

INKUBATOR
BOOKS

Published by Inkubator Books
www.inkubatorbooks.com

ISBN (eBook): 978-1-83756-003-5
ISBN (Paperback): 978-1-83756-004-2
ISBN (Hardback): 978-1-83756-005-9

1

Sometimes, it's just better not to feel anything, Emily thought.

It wasn't a mantra that she wanted to live her life by, but at a time like now, it was hard to deny its efficacy and appeal. Emily was devastated, and she felt like her heart was going to bleed out of her chest. Her eyes felt dry and painful despite being unable to stop crying.

It was, quite frankly, a bit of a day.

It had started off well enough, as far as her days went. The night before, she'd finished an evening shift that bled into the late shift at her waitressing job. It had been the seventh night in a row that she had worked, and she was grateful that she was finally going to have a night off. Frankly, most of the people who came to dine at the upper-class restaurant where she worked were fine. They spoke politely and tipped well. They rarely brought along loud children or a failing date. When she was working the floor and serving her patrons, everything was pretty good.

The problem largely stemmed from management. Her

overworked boss just wanted his restaurant to survive during hard times and wasn't interested in making friends with his employees. And as such, he didn't care if his serving staff were tired, needed sick days, or needed a night off to study for their exams.

She spent most of her nights tired, fed up, and frankly, somewhat desperate for cash, so she was very willing to put up with all of it.

In her day life, Emily occasionally made a little side money working as a virtual assistant. Effectively, she worked as a secretary for no particular company. She didn't have a desk or an office to travel to. She simply serviced the administrative work of anybody willing to hire her online, and she performed her duties using her laptop in her apartment.

Emily wasn't particularly surprised when she realized that being a virtual assistant—and a self-employed, self-marketing virtual assistant at that—wasn't going to pay the bills. Which was why she spent her days collating and assembling paperwork and her nights working as a waitress in an upscale restaurant for meager pay, which was justified by the fact that she worked in a job where she earned tips . . . but management forced her to distribute said tips in a pool. She worked hard, but she scraped by.

She was astounded that she even had a boyfriend, considering all the time she spent away from him.

Which, in a roundabout way, brought her back to all the crying.

She had started dating Jeremy in college. They lived together, pooling their resources so they would be able to afford an apartment in Edmonton. He worked in an auto dealership, largely off a biweekly paycheck but occasionally —in all honesty, very rarely—on commission. He was a pretty cool guy when they started dating and remained a pretty cool guy throughout the few years they'd been together. Lately, though, he'd been growing somewhat distant, his words becoming very habitual, his actions somewhat repetitive. It always seemed as if he only said the least that he had to, and then he was off, going to work or staying late for work.

Emily blamed herself.

In a wider sense, Emily also blamed the economy due to the fact that she had to work all these jobs just to be able to buy groceries and pay her half of the rent. But those arguments could only go so far. At the end of the day, regardless of who was to blame, Emily thought that she was choosing to use up all her time at work and provide none for her boyfriend. They saw each other in the mornings, of course. She would sometimes send him texts, and they would usually be able to meet up at the apartment in the evening. Assuming one of them wasn't already asleep by the time the other one got home.

That said, the times that they found themselves in the apartment, awake and at the same time, were getting fewer and further between. And the texts never seemed to be replied to anymore.

Emily was starting to worry that Jeremy was going to break up with her. It seemed very possible, given the little amount of time they had for each other. She never could actually find the time to make something special just for the two of them. And by all accounts, Jeremy seemed to have given up trying to find that kind of time between them. There was always so much work, always so much exhaustion these days.

But she had to try. She had to try to keep it a stable relationship, if for no other reason than simply to be able to feel like she'd accomplished something in her life. If she didn't have a boyfriend, if she wasn't heading toward a long-term

relationship, then really, what was she doing? She'd gradu-
ated from college and, what, ended up being a waitress? With
a barely existent side gig? And she was going to do that for
the rest of her life, just scrape by in jobs she hated to earn
enough money to pay off her rent every month along the way
until, eventually, she grew so old that she was forced to retire
with nothing to show for it except forty to fifty years of rent
payments? What was the point? What was the point of any
of it?

Emily needed to believe that there was some kind of
partner in her life, somebody who trusted and loved her. She
needed to have something to show for constantly struggling
every day, trying to achieve something.

Despite the difficulties, she needed to make this relationship work.

Today, of all days, she finally had a night off from her
waitressing job. She was going to stay in, catch up on some
virtual administrative work, and have a lovely evening with
Jeremy. She would talk to him, see how he was doing, maybe
even apologize to him for not being so readily available all
the time like she used to be, like in the earlier days.

And then . . .

Earlier, she had gotten up from the tedious data entry
filing she'd been doing—it seemed like a lifetime ago now,
barely even important—and went off to the kitchen to get a
glass of water. Along the way, she glanced over at the front
door to the apartment.

There was a sheet of paper on the floor. Somebody had
slipped it underneath the door.

She picked it up and noticed it was handwritten. Somebody had scrawled on the page:

He's been seeing some blonde woman behind your back.

Okay, creepy enough on its own.

Then she flipped the page over.

It was a photo, probably taken with a smart phone. It was printed out on paper, so it wasn't printed professionally onto a photo-quality glossy sheet. Somebody just ran it through a standard printer. The quality looked slapdash.

But more important were the contents of the photo.

There was Jeremy, his hand around the waist of some blonde woman. He was smiling at her. With desire in his eyes.

And she, looking back at him equally amorously, had her hands on his shoulders. The photo seemed to have been taken a moment before they were about to kiss. Happily. Right out in public, in the middle of the street.

Like a young couple in love.

Her first thought was that this was some kind of sick joke. That somebody was just trying to hurt her or hurt her relationship. Except she couldn't think of anybody who would do this to her. She barely knew anybody in the building, and it wouldn't be easy for anybody who wasn't a resident to break in. Also, she and Jeremy weren't social, so it wasn't like a lot of people knew about their relationship. And on top of that, if Emily was being completely honest with herself, she didn't really have that many friends to begin with. She didn't socialize with anybody at the restaurant, and her virtual assistant job had turned her into a bit of a loner.

So who would even know to do this?

At first glance, the photo appeared to be legitimate. No sign of Photoshopping.

And she recognized the shirt he was wearing from their closet. He very rarely wore it. It was a little on the flashy side, cute, but not really appropriate for his job.

In fact, the only time she could remember his wearing it to work was that day when he didn't come back at all. He'd said he had to work late and that he was spending the night at a friend's house.

This was legit.

Her imagination ran wild. There were a lot of late nights, a lot of nights when Jeremy would show up and go straight to bed, so she wouldn't even see him until they woke up together.

All the time they'd been living together, she'd never invaded his privacy. Never looked through his things. She felt it was the least she could do to honor the spirit of their relationship. Especially considering she didn't live up to the actions of it and never could be a good girlfriend.

But this photo . . .

Barely thirty minutes later, she had searched through all his stuff in their mutual bedroom. Many of his pants had notes in them that he had left in there from when this other girl gave them to him. Mostly insipid love notes, some with a phone number or directions to get to a certain bar. Some of them were just little suggestive things, like lipstick kisses.

Looking through his shirts, she saw there were some lipstick stains on the collars. They didn't match any color that she normally wore.

He'd obviously been seeing somebody.

Then it all made sense. Why he'd been distant. Why he couldn't care less.

Because he had already moved on. He just didn't want to move out in the process. He didn't have the guts to actually end the current relationship with Emily.

He had destroyed everything.

And Emily certainly felt destroyed.

Her computer kept dinging in the background somewhere. Evidently, some of her clients wanted responses to their emails and didn't understand why she wasn't as prompt as she usually was. She half-heartedly approached the computer in the hopes of being able to work through it.

But just the thought of it . . . She was going to be working at the computer the rest of her life. This was all she had left. She wasn't good enough to be able to hold onto a relationship.

She didn't matter, she thought. She didn't matter.

And so, the crying. The screaming. The frustration about all those years of work that amounted to nothing.

Now she called Chandra, her old college roommate, whom she still called her friend, even though they barely had time to socialize. Thankfully, Chandra wasn't going to act as if distance was a deciding factor between them. She'd always been Emily's friend.

That was something Emily believed in.

Emily told her friend about the note.

"It's pretty damning," Chandra said. "I guess it all comes down to whether it's true or not."

Emily understood why Chandra was being careful with her words. But she wasn't necessarily happy about it. She wasn't sure of exactly what she wanted right now. She was too distraught. Given what she was going through, it was far easier to determine what it was that she didn't want. And she didn't want to be consoled and told that everything was going to be all right. She didn't want to believe it, either.

She didn't want a lot of things right now. She didn't really want anything.

Sometimes, it's just better not to feel anything, she thought again.

"If it's not true," Emily managed to say between sobs, "then who the fuck would do this? Who would Photoshop this? And why Jeremy? Why would they send it to me?"

"I really can't think of anything," Chandra said. "I'm sorry."

She was sorry, Emily thought while covering her eyes with her hand. Everybody was going to be sorry for her. Thank God she didn't have to go to work tonight. She couldn't imagine being able to handle it. She was a pathetic wreck, somebody who deserved pity.

"I've got to go see him," Emily said.

"Go?" asked Chandra. "Go where?"

"We share a phone account," Emily replied. "I'm able to detect where his phone signal is coming from."

"Oh! You, uh, never used it before to, well, check on him or—"

"I never felt I had to, Chandra."

"Right, right. But what's the point? Can't you just wait for him to get home?"

"And do what, ask him to leave? This is our place. He shouldn't leave. I shouldn't leave. But I don't wanna stay here with him."

"You can come to my parents' place. I don't know how they'll feel about it, but I don't want you to be homeless tonight if you can't stay in your own place."

Emily smiled a little through the tears. Chandra, after graduating college, had moved back in with her parents. She wasn't doing financially well herself. She had nothing to offer, and despite that, she offered everything she could. She was glad she had somebody like Chandra in her life.

"Thank you," Emily replied. "I might have to do that. But also, I want to confirm that it's true. I mean, he's out late again. He's probably with her."

"Yeah," Chandra replied weakly. She sounded like she wanted to add something else before just repeating, "Yeah."

After disconnecting, Emily grabbed her keys, jacket, and the photo, then checked her phone. Evidently, Jeremy had gone to a bar in Legal, a small town about thirty miles away.

His job had no reason to send him there. And he said he'd be working late tonight, as he usually did.

There really wasn't anything in Legal other than a small suburban community, which also had a fairly decent bar. A good way to get drunk and meet up discreetly.

The less she thought about it, the better.

The less she felt, the better.

2

_____

Nighttime was quickly approaching. In a few hours, it would be pitch black. Emily rarely drove out of town in this direction, owing to the fact that she didn't know anybody out here and had no reason to go to Legal. As such, she didn't know what the night sky looked like out this far. In Edmonton, there was always some kind of nightlife, always some sports arena or bars open somewhere, meaning the night sky would be blocked out by all the lights.

She wondered if, going out this far, the sky would be riddled with stars. By all accounts, it probably should be. Or maybe the air was too filthy here, or maybe the lights from nearby surrounding farmhouses from the rural regions would help to mask it all. Maybe, under other circumstances, she could come out here and see the stars.

Maybe, Emily thought, under different circumstances, she could've come out here with Jeremy to enjoy a starry night sky illuminated only by the moonlight. It would've seemed so romantic.

Maybe, under different circumstances, she wouldn't be toiling every hour of her life just to make a little bit of money.

And therefore, maybe she would've had the time to be able to spend with him and make the relationship work. Maybe they wouldn't have grown apart while living together.

Or maybe Jeremy wouldn't be the kind of person who would cheat on his girlfriend. Who would find some other woman to shack up with behind her back. Who wouldn't lie about having to work long hours at the auto dealership when, in fact, he was going a county over to meet up with some chick in a bar somewhere.

Maybe, just maybe, if everything had worked out exactly the way that it hadn't, then life would've been different. Obviously enough.

She didn't know why she was thinking these thoughts. She didn't have a fabricated fictional life where everything was magical and wonderful and everything worked out for her. Emily simply had the life that she did. Finding meaningful work after college was hard, making her question what the point of going to college was in the first place if it wasn't really going to amount to much. Having a romantic interest wasn't a dream ride a hundred percent of the time. It was a lot of work as well. And she didn't put that work in. And a guy wasn't automatically some sort of dream goal just because she fell in love with him. Sometimes, when they wanted to end a relationship, instead of doing the right thing and simply ending it, the guy kept it going, cheating on his girlfriend behind her back. In all likelihood, probably just to keep the apartment.

Apparently, Emily realized, betraying her and hurting her was easier than the difficulty of having to move residence. How wonderful.

The only noise coming from anywhere was the sound of the wheels driving along the highway. It was a paved road, but it wasn't kept up on a constant basis, as there were cracks and various bits of road debris here and there, making things louder and bumpier as she drove along. At least it was a reasonably wide highway, so she had some options. She would hate the thought of having to drive along some gravel road in the middle of the night. Despite how beautiful it must be to see the stars, going out into the countryside this late at night provided some horrifying thoughts. The prospect of getting stuck out here, so far from the civilization she knew, scared her. She didn't want the sound of her car driving along the highway to remind her that she was the only one out here.

As such, she turned on the radio. She really wasn't in the mood to listen to any kind of music or even hear voices. She just didn't have the heart to feel like being a part of anything right now. She was certain she would despise anything she heard. She also didn't want to risk the possibility of associating a song she might've liked with this day, of all days, when she learned that her boyfriend was cheating on her. And of course, God help her if she ended up hitting a station that was playing one of those insipid breakup songs, the kind that gloried in and celebrated how sad everybody was.

There were certainly a lot of country music channels in the region, so the possibility of hitting one of those types of songs wasn't outside the realm of possibility.

Nevertheless, she needed to hear something right now. Anything that might even have a hope of getting her mind off what she was doing. She knew she had to get to Legal. She knew she had to track down Jeremy's phone signal, confront him, and get the truth out of him. She just didn't want it to be the only thing on her mind.

She turned on the radio, and of course, the first thing that was playing with some classic rock song that she vaguely recognized from a popular band but hadn't heard in years. It wasn't even a favorite of hers, so there was a point in her favor. At least she wouldn't have to remember it.

It did its job of making her forget about all of this until, eventually, it started fading away toward the end of the song and moving on to the beats of the local news station's information service.

A loud stinger, followed by a voice crying out, *"News break!"* and then, *"This is Tracy Galloway, and good evening, this is your news break for tonight. In our top story, all the major opposition federal leaders are calling for the dismissal of famed financial advisor Michael Keating after increasing pressure in regard to his recent sex scandal in which not only did he engage in an extramarital affair, but he also may have compromised the integrity of our nation's security by bringing his financial work home with him, only to have it stolen by the woman with whom he had been having the affair."*

Emily's jaw dropped. The timing couldn't have been worse. She was vaguely aware of the story somewhere in the back of her mind, but given her busy schedule, she'd just relegated it to more national news, along with all the other stuff she barely knew about. But now, of all days, and in regard to all the things that she'd been going through in the last hour, did the first news story she heard really have to be about a man cheating on his wife? Granted, the news story continued focusing on the financial scandal aspect of it all—now that she knew what the story was, she tried to block it out and sort of relegate it to the background—but all she could hear was how a man was cheating on his wife. How did the universe just choose to remind her about how infidelity worked, about her own situation, about pouring all of this down upon her shoulders?

The universe really wanted to rub it in now, didn't it?

Emily found herself flooring the gas pedal. Maybe she would be caught by some hidden police car radar, or maybe she would crash into a tree. She didn't care. It didn't matter anymore. She just wanted it all to stop.

The pain of feeling. Of having to feel anything.

In a strange way, having to hear any kind of background noise rather than the reminder of the wheels on pavement, driving her to her destination, had a certain way of being comforting. So she wasn't about to turn off the station, all things considered. Rather, she just continued listening as it switched to provincial news and then started talking about sports. Apparently, some baseball team was doing really well against some other baseball team, and a lot of people were either happy or disappointed about it.

She was never really much into sports, and now, that news just seemed so narcissistically unnecessary to listen to.

Another stinger sounded, followed by *"Entertainment news!"* And then, *"For the past six weeks now, the latest offering from the cinematic superhero universe has been topping box office sales, and it's starting to look like it'll run on for another week despite competition from the new rom-com* New York Studio *making a dent in their profit margins. A lot of attention has been drawn to the stars of the new romantic comedy, Mason Taylor and Zefia Gohanagutsheir, who it has been reported in the rumor mill might be a real couple both on and off camera. People are wondering, however, if these are just rumors being pushed by studio executives, hoping to entice people to see the movie and see the couple in action."*

Emily was genuinely starting to wonder whether it was a good idea to turn on the radio. It was starting to seem as if everybody in the universe was either cheating or deeply in love. She wondered if radio news was always like this, and given the emotional turmoil she was going through at the time, this was simply the first time she'd ever really paid attention to it. Or maybe it was all a coincidence.

Or maybe she really was a failure where others had succeeded. Maybe she really was the stepping-stone others used to move forward in their lives.

She cried some more. In the best possible light, the news reports were insipid.

The entertainment news continued for another half minute before providing another musical stinger, followed by *"Local news!"* And then, *"Horror rang out among some of the residents in a West Edmonton neighborhood when it was discovered that an abandoned and unused dumpster near a recycling center was actually being used as a storage area for several humans' remains. Police were quick to coordinate the area after a local recycling representative began reporting odors coming from the old dumpster. Our news team was able to question the police and learned that there were at least three victims, long dead, left on the property. However, only one has been identified—the body of Cynthia Richards, whom this station had reported as missing almost a month ago. Sources at the crime scene indicate that the police were able to identify the body, as it was the only one that still had legal identification on their person in the form of a driver's license. This community, which had been brought together in the search for the missing Cynthia Richards, is now brought together to comfort each other as the daughter of one of their neighbors has been found dead. Representatives of the West Edmonton community have requested that memorials be left near the location where the body was found, and the family requests to be left to mourn privately and in peace."*

Emily shivered. She remembered, vaguely, hearing about Cynthia Richards's story about a month ago. There were a lot of requests for volunteers to help search for the body, just in case she wound up dead, although the family hadn't given up hope that she was simply kidnapped or had run off somewhere. Emily tried not to think about it. It was tragic, of course, but in her mind, it was just another story of a woman being taken in the middle of the night and disappearing, probably at the hands of some asshole who couldn't take a rejection.

And now that she had been found in a dumpster, maybe Emily was right.

It was already dangerous for women to be out alone at night. She had to wrestle with that thought constantly, seeing as how she had to go from her job to her car in the early hours of the morning sometimes. God help her when some asshole decided to hide out in the parking lot and jump her as she was putting her key into her door.

Just another reason for her to be grateful that she was in a steady relationship. No matter how dark the world got, no matter how evil everything seemed, at least she knew that she could always count on the love of her life being there for her. At least she knew she could go home to a happy relationship.

A happy relationship, she thought. She shook her head, trying to shake off the headache she'd been nursing for hours now. She'd thought she was in a happy relationship with Jeremy for God knew how long. Meanwhile, she rarely ever saw him anymore.

And he had given up on her quite some time ago. What a naïve idiot she was.

She rounded a corner and came onto the main highway that entered Legal, a quaint little community. She wasn't sure that it had any kind of industry supporting it. It was probably one of those old towns that, at one point in history, depended on its connection to the railways for all the farmers, but now, generations later, with all the farmers being able to transport their crops using their own trucks, this little place just became a hideaway for wealthy suburbanites. That, or broke laborers who couldn't afford to live in the city.

At the very least, it seemed nice. They had a country bakery, now closed this late in the evening. There was a grocery store that was closed as well, a strange sight, since she had more experience with grocery stores being open well into the late hours.

And then she saw it. The only business that, in a community this small, was still open after seven and would probably be open well until sunrise.

The local bar. Looked like a little country place. Looked a little seedy as well.

It was hard to imagine why Jeremy would drive all this way just for a girl to cheat on Emily with, but then again, it was hard to imagine any of this happening at all. All the same, when she looked at her phone, it indicated that Jeremy's phone signal was emanating from a few dozen feet away, inside the building. He was definitely in there.

And looking over to the side, her heart sank as she saw it.

There, in the parking lot of the business, was Jeremy's car.

So for what it was worth, at least that part of it was true. He really did drive all the way out here. It wasn't some sort of technical error, and his phone wasn't stolen. Jeremy was actually here. In this far-off, distant country bar, in the middle of the night, lying to Emily about working late hours at the auto dealership.

Going back to her own car behind her, she grabbed the crumpled-up photo of Jeremy and the blonde woman smiling at each other happily from the backseat of her car.

She told herself this would all be over soon. She wasn't exactly sure what she was thinking about because she knew full well that the pain would linger on for much, much longer.

3

E mily walked into the bar and wasn't really surprised by what she saw. It was a typical small-town bar, complete with far too much wood paneling and timber used to construct the bar, the tables, chairs, and anything else that didn't have to be metal or glass. And the lighting was poor, and that seem to be the way everybody liked it. A few people in the bar seemed to want to keep to themselves, enjoy a beer, and based on the haze of the smoke in the air, a couple of cigarettes. Emily never frequented these kinds of places and had to think for a second whether it was in fact illegal to smoke in bars in this area. She suspected that the owners of the establishment probably didn't care.

To her left was a table where a single, slightly nerdy-looking man sat nursing a beer, eyeing her. Probably the first time he'd seen a woman on her own in ages. He really did look out of place in an environment that seemed to cater to the image of the gun-toting machismo. From that table, she scanned around and saw a few tables occupied by dudes hanging out, enjoying a beer, letting their stomachs rest on the table in some cases. At the far end of the room, some men and women enjoyed a game of pool. Past the bar to her right was a stairwell that led upward. Emily thought it was probably the stairs that led to the motel that was attached to this bar. She saw a woman with a hiked-up leather dress giggling and smiling at a larger man, heavily bearded and wearing his plaid hunting gear, as she held his hand and pulled him up the stairs.

She didn't have any proof that this man had rented a prostitute, and she certainly didn't want to stereotype the woman, but at the same time, she wasn't naïve. She was just wondering if maybe Jeremy and his blonde girl were up there right now.

But it wasn't quite as bad as that. Looking over to the bar, she saw them. There was a blonde college girl sitting on a stool, her hand around a beer, chatting happily. In front of her, with his back turned to Emily, was Jeremy. She couldn't see his face, but she recognized that hair and those broad shoulders. She'd spent a year waking up next to them daily.

Only for it all to come to this.

She marched over. She roughly tapped her finger on Jeremy's shoulder. She felt like a disapproving mother when she did so, but she couldn't think of any other way to get his attention.

The blonde chick looked confused and defensively protective.

Jeremy simply turned around, looking confused and annoyed at being interrupted. Then he realized who was facing him. "Emily," he said, startled, "what are you doing here?"

"What am I doing here?" she replied. "What are *you* doing here?"

Jeremy froze, the look on his face slowly filling with incredulity, but he was still largely confused. He looked like she genuinely did not understand what he was saying. "No, seriously, what are you doing here?" he asked again. "Like, how did you get up here? Wait, why are you here?"

Emily didn't need this, and she felt like she wanted to grab the nearest thing and bash it across Jeremy's head. She had literally walked in on him out on a date with some strange woman, and he was acting as if she'd inconvenienced him.

"I drove up here, you asshole," she cried. "Why are you even here? Who is this? Why are you here with her?"

Jeremy glanced at the blonde woman. "This is a friend from work. We just went out to relax after work. It was a hard day."

"You went out? To relax? You drove up here to Legal? You went to the next town, half an hour out of Edmonton, for a beer. This is where you go? For a beer?"

"I got tired of the same thing back home. I wanted to try something new."

"Yeah, I bet you did."

"Hell is that supposed to mean?"

"Oh, God," the blonde woman finally said, rolling her eyes. "Is this your regular girl you're cheating on?"

Jeremy turned his head sharply, looking right at the woman who finally spoke. He stared at her, wide-eyed, practically begging her to shut up.

"What?" asked Emily.

"I mean," the blonde woman continued, "it wasn't that hard to figure out. He never said he had somebody, but he's not that good at hiding it. Your picture is all over the apartment. So is your stuff."

Jeremy leaned his head back and slapped his open palm down on his eyes. "Jesus Christ, Erica," he murmured. "Why now?"

"So you knew?" Emily asked the blonde woman, who was evidently named Erica.

"I mean, yeah. I figured it out. He obviously didn't tell me, but he wasn't exactly hiding it, was he?"

"But you continued to go out with him."

"Yeah."

"You just kept seeing him? You didn't ask him about me or try to find out?"

"I don't care. I'm having a good time with him. Why ruin a good thing?" Erica shrugged and took another sip of her beer. Over the rim of the bottle, she gave this look to Emily, like she was annoyed, like she was putting up with having to read college homework that she couldn't have given two shits about.

This chick wasn't scared of Emily. She wasn't even embarrassed. She was actually looking down at her. Emily couldn't believe it.

She turned to Jeremy, trying to see if any of this was real, if he was going to try to sputter his way out of this with lies or some sort of explanation that would fix everything.

Instead, he lifted his head and swung his stool around to face Emily. "Look," he said, not willing to meet her gaze. "I didn't want you to find out this way, but . . . fuck it. It's over between us. Has been for a while." Then he shrugged. And he still wouldn't look Emily in the eyes.

"What?" she replied. Emily couldn't think of anything else to say. Couldn't think of much, really.

"I mean," Jeremy finally said after a long silence, "I don't know what to tell you. I just don't wanna do it anymore."

"You're . . . you're just . . . Like, do you even care? You've been seeing her behind my back! Don't you even care?"

"See, that's what I'm talking about," Jeremy said, pointing his finger at Emily. "This right here? This is what I don't need. Like, it's really straightforward. I don't want to see you, it's over, and I don't know what else you're expecting from this."

"You've been lying to me and cheating on me, and you're treating me like I'm the bad guy."

"Jesus Christ, Emily, there is no 'bad guy'. It's just over. I tried to see you as sexy. I tried to see you as, I don't know, appealing. But I can't give two shits about you. You're boring. You're not cool. I mean, when we started dating, I kind of liked the young, innocent, submissive thing, but I just thought that was a college thing. I didn't think you'd be boring the rest of your life. I don't wanna wake up every morning and look at you and think to myself, *what the fuck did I do to myself?* for all of forever. Do you even want to see yourself every morning in the mirror? Think about it."

Emily felt the rage building up in her throat. He was actually doing this. He was actually telling her that the reason he was breaking up with her was because he didn't wanna try anymore. And that he was entitled to. That he just got bored with her and wanted to move on. But more than that, the fact that he just couldn't give a shit. That he simply, blatantly, just outright didn't care. If she hadn't stumbled upon him, if she had never found out about any of this, he would've continued to see this chick behind her back. He was comfortable with it.

And now, being confronted with his infidelity, he was comfortable with this as well. He was comfortable with the idea of moving on without her.

He couldn't care less. He was disposing of her. Offhandedly. Like trash.

Emily looked over Jeremy's shoulder, seeing if there was any reaction from Erica. If anything, she seemed to be gleeful.

"Hey, don't look at me," she replied, throwing up her hands. "I'm not a part of this. I was going out with him before, and I'll be going out with him now."

The anger she felt rising in her throat was beginning to turn into full-on rage. None of this was going the way she wanted it to. She wasn't exactly sure what she wanted from this confrontation, but she knew it wasn't this. She knew she didn't want to be treated like an annoyance, like she was wrong to have learned about any of this.

She could still feel the crumpled-up printout of Jeremy's infidelity in her hand. It was like it had come to nothing, like whoever left it for her had been playing her for a fool.

"Look," Jeremy finally said, rubbing his eyes as if he just wanted all this nonsense to be over. "I really think you should move out."

The rage in her throat wasn't willing to be contained anymore. "*I* should move out?" Emily said, raising her voice.

"Well, yeah. I mean . . . where would I go? And besides, think about it. I make more money than you. Like, you couldn't afford it on your own."

"I'm not going anywhere!" Emily screamed at the top of her lungs. She had now attracted the attention of everybody at the bar. She didn't care. She also got these two idiots to react to her, finally. And that was all that mattered. "Why should I go anywhere? That's *my* apartment. I didn't do anything wrong."

And with that, Emily grabbed a nearby barstool and flung it across the room toward the windows on the opposite end. She missed, but she knew there were plenty more barstools where that came from.

She didn't care about what she was doing or how it looked. She wanted to smash Jeremy's head in. She wanted to smash in the pretty face of this bimbo. But since she would never have the guts to do it, she knew she wanted to destroy everything else in the world. She wanted it to burn.

"Jesus Christ, you fucking nutcase," Erica said, leaping out of her seat. She then turned to anybody who would listen to her, pointing at Emily and crying out, "She's crazy! She's fucking insane!"

"Fuck is wrong with you?" cried Jeremy.

Emily smashed another barstool on a table next to her. "What the fuck do you think is wrong with me?" She grabbed some glass mugs and threw them across the room. Other patrons had to duck and dodge out of the way. "I have wasted everything on you!"

The bartender tried to grab her.

Emily punched her in the face. "Why is this happening to me?" She glanced around. She had caused a scene and lots of public damage. She had caused the bartender to fall back and hit her head on a wooden post. She didn't seem seriously injured, but strictly speaking, it was still assault. If the cops were called over now, she would be in a prison cell.

Everything was going horribly wrong. None of this was the way it should be.

"Fuck you." Emily crumpled up the note and threw it at Jeremy. "You can keep this stupid picture that was shoved under the door. You ruined my life. I'm not going anywhere. You move in with your new girlfriend."

Jeremy looked like he was trying to restrain a laugh as he caught the note and smoothed it out. "What?" he asked, smiling as he looked at the photo.

Behind him, Erica shook her head and smiled. "I remember that day."

Emily started crying. She had made her point, even if she didn't feel that he was about to do anything. Or even if she felt she didn't understand it herself. For what it was worth, she'd made it.

She had just been dumped. And now . . . there was nothing left to say.

She turned on her heel and headed toward the door. Somewhere behind her, a few bar patrons applauded her, weakly, but not with any heart behind it. For the most part, everybody in the bar seemed to just be in shock.

All except that guy who had been seated at a table near the door, apparently. As she approached the exit, he came toward her and firmly grabbed Emily by the shoulders, stopping her in her tracks.

"Hey," he said. "I seem to have lost my number. Can I have yours?"

It took Emily a moment to realize what the hell was happening. She had just finished being humiliated by her now ex-boyfriend not five seconds earlier. "What?"

"Well, now you got to give me your number. That's how it works."

Emily had no damn clue who this guy was or what he was doing, but she still thought the police might show up at any moment, so she tried to force her way past him toward the door.

She felt a tug on her arm as this guy violently pulled her back to where she was when he stopped her.

"Oh, come on," he whined. "Just give me your number. You'll never know what I'm like until you try, right?"

"Get the fuck away from me, you little creep!"

"Fuck you," he said. "You just got dumped by some loser. I'm trying to help you feel better. What, women don't appreciate shit anymore?"

Emily could feel her hand curling into a claw, as if she were turning into some raging animal. "I am sick and tired of being told by some dude that there is something wrong with me, or that I'm crazy, or that this is all my fucking fault. I don't need you. Get away from me. I am not getting picked up by some guy right now. I didn't come to this bar for you, you narcissistic creep." And with that, she ripped her arm from his grip and blasted for the door.

Somewhere out of the corner of her eye, she was sure she saw the creepy guy smiling.

Probably laughing at her.

4

Emily was fully aware of the dark reality of having to be a woman alone at night in a bar environment. She had certainly gone through self-defense courses and learned all of the tricks and trades. But she was also aware, back in the depths of her mind, that learning about something and actually having to experience it were sometimes very different matters indeed.

Case in point, she stepped out of the bar, looked out at the world around her, and realized she was in a pretty dangerous situation.

Firstly, she was a woman alone at night. It wasn't like she hadn't been alone at night before, but she was always aware that the world wasn't very kind to women in dangerous situations, even if they had every right to be there. Every time she was alone at night, she had to remind herself that yes, she was always capable of being potentially threatened.

A lifetime of experiences as a woman had taught her to go through the media checklist of everything she needed to know in order to be . . . well, maybe not safe, but comparatively safer.

She looked around her in all directions. There wasn't anybody else around as far as she could see. At the very least, this area was one of the few parts of town that seemed to have streetlights, so she had a pretty good range of vision. It was apparent that the only other buildings within sight were nearby residences.

Which, by association, led her to the second point on her checklist. She was in a small town. Out of her depth.

If she were out at night back in Edmonton, she could go down any street and expect to see streetlights all over the place, other businesses to run inside. She knew where all the local police stations were. But this? This wasn't her town. If there were some hiding place for some creep to jump out of, she would never know it.

She reached into her jacket pocket and grabbed her car keys. From long experience, she knew to position one in between her knuckles in case she needed to throw a punch with a little extra edge.

As she considered her situation, the most immediate danger she could think of was from the bar behind her. That jackass who'd tried to stop her and hit on her—if one could even call it that—was probably still in there, either fantasizing about her or berating her. There was always a very realistic possibility that he could just hop out and try to take her from behind or something. At the very least, hop out and call her a bitch.

That was why she stood so close to the bar door when she left. He would have to open a door to get out to meet her. She didn't want to give him that possibility. She wanted to be able to hold the door or possibly hide the moment he exited. It was an extreme risk, she knew, but it was preferable to giving him a wide berth and letting him use it to his advantage.

The other element still inside that bar was, of course, her boyfriend.

Or . . . she had to get used to the idea of thinking of him as her now ex-boyfriend.

Jeremy and his cheating bitch. The one who found out about her "boyfriend's" infidelity at the same time Emily confronted him with it and seemed to be perfectly fine. She seemed a little buzzed and a little too proud to be a young college girl. So Emily wasn't surprised if she felt very high and mighty of herself and her prowess. She was just a little astounded that she didn't even try to hide it.

And even more astounded that Jeremy, once finally caught, wasn't embarrassed at all. He clearly couldn't care less.

Emily wasn't sure how she left the two of them. She knew she was upset, and she wanted nothing more to do with either of them. But she also knew that after screaming up a storm, she wasn't really paying that much attention to what had actually happened between her and her now ex-boyfriend. It was hard to imagine that he would go back to his seat and continue drinking with his new girl, but then again, there was no reason to believe that he would've just accepted the fact that he had been caught, but that was how it turned out anyway. The whole thing was rather unbelievable.

So maybe her ex-boyfriend and his new woman were still there, drinking away. Or maybe they were upstairs fucking. Or maybe they snuck out the back door and went home to fuck now that he didn't have anything left to hide and he insisted that the apartment should be his, anyway.

Emily threw her head back. Of course, that was another factor to consider. The apartment. That was the only place she had to go. She wasn't sure if Jeremy had anywhere else to go either. There was always the possibility of kicking him out and making him live with his new woman, but if she really was as young as she seemed, then maybe she lived in a dorm on campus. Bringing some old guy along to crash in your dorm was certainly frowned upon. Unless Jeremy had somewhere else to go, he would probably end up back in her home.

Their home.

Emily realized that if he was truly as selfish and sadistic as he seemed to be this evening, then perhaps he would drive home and change the locks on her, effectively locking her out of her own home. And then where would she go? Chandra's place? That was an option. But she didn't want to impose on her friend.

After all, Emily had done nothing wrong. She'd just put her trust in a man who didn't deserve her, as far as she was concerned. She deserved to live in that apartment more than him, more so than anybody else. She wasn't willing to give up on it.

And so she knew what she had to do—hop back into her car, race back to Edmonton, and hunker down in her apartment. Make sure that she would be there and make it clear that she wasn't going anywhere. Not tonight, not any night.

She quickly contemplated the possibility of having to live with her ex-boyfriend for an extended period of time. Or possibly, having to lose her waitressing job so she didn't give him the opportunity of catching her out of the apartment.

Emily shook her head. How had her life come to this?

Well, she thought, *no time like the present.* She went over to her car, unlocked it, but realized that she had never locked it in the first place. She slid behind the wheel, turned the key . . .

And got no result.

She couldn't get a sound out of her ignition. Or at least, not an engine starting sound. When she turned the key, it sounded as if it was trying to accomplish something, but there was no electricity lighting anything. Something was off.

It was like there was no connection between the ignition and the engine.

Emily pulled the key back and gave it another turn, trying to force it to come on. Nothing.

She put the key back in again and tried to start the engine once more. She kept that key turned for a very long time this time, longer than necessary in order to get the engine to start up. She was starting to wonder if she might end up flooding the engine.

But she wasn't hearing anything other than the ignition's click. She wasn't even sure there was any gas going into the engine.

She reached down and yanked on the red hood release, then stepped out of the car and pulled the hood up to take a look inside.

It took her a whole ten seconds of staring at the contraption that was her engine before she had to concede that she had no idea how to find the problem or even contemplate fixing it. All she knew was that she couldn't get the engine to work.

Did it fail on the way here? she wondered. That wasn't possible, or at least probable, since the car had been driving nice and fine on the way to Legal. How long had she been in the bar? Five or ten minutes at most? How did the entire car just fail in that time? Did she overwork it driving here so fast?

Emily thought it over and realized that it made the most sense. She had been speeding in order to get to the bar as quickly as possible, simply to confirm what she already suspected. Sure seemed like a big waste now, having a clunker of a car that wouldn't even start.

Getting back into the safety of her car, Emily pulled out her phone to call an auto service to get a tow.

She went to her online app to find the phone number for

a towing service and proceeded to watch as her internet provider struggled to load.

She kept watching the little wheel on her screen spin around, struggling to find an internet signal. And nothing. No results.

She pulled up her general settings and tried to see if she could connect to an internet service that way, but there wasn't any kind of service at all. Not internet, not even mobile. The entire phone had become incapable of collecting or transmitting any kind of data.

She had lost all contact to the outside world.

After staring at her phone helplessly for several more minutes, she leaned back in her seat and contemplated the situation. She wasn't sure if the bar had a landline. Logically, any good bar would. That said, she had nearly knocked out the bartender and had caused a general disturbance in the establishment. She couldn't even begin to imagine having to go back in there and request to use the landline to call for a taxi or a tow. In all likelihood, the moment they saw her come back in, they would probably use that landline to call the police.

They were probably calling the police on her right now. And if that were true, then it was only a matter of time before they came to get her.

Maybe they would help her in her desperate situation. But considering the amount of damage she'd caused in the bar, they would probably "help her" by arresting her and taking her to a cell somewhere.

Even if that wasn't the case, what else did she have as an option in that bar? Asking Jeremy for help? The same Jeremy who'd basically told her to get lost and move out? That wasn't a very realistic or appealing prospect in her mind.

She looked around the neighborhood. It was late at night now. Was she really supposed to start knocking on doors and asking to use a phone? Any sensible homeowner, especially in a small town, wouldn't open the door to a stranger this late at night. Plus, she was also putting her own safety in their hands. She was so far from her comfort zone.

She didn't really have any options left.

So that's that, she thought. No phone, no car, no way of contacting the outside world, and if she stayed in the car, eventually, the police would round her up.

Add to that another factor that Emily suddenly realized. If the police weren't already here by now, odds were, the little town of Legal didn't have its own police department and probably had to depend on the county sheriff. Which, while beneficial at the immediate moment, also gave her another idea that she didn't enjoy thinking of.

If there wasn't an officer in the area to round her up . . . then strictly speaking, the roads were clear to her.

She could go for it. She could hitchhike all the way back down to Edmonton. She already knew how to get there, having driven this way. She just had to walk the same way back in reverse.

Along a dark rural highway. In the middle of nowhere. Alone. Ready to be assaulted by any psycho or wild animal that came her way.

Or wait here to get a criminal record and possibly jail time, since she certainly didn't have enough spare money to post bail.

She hated the situation. She hated having to be put in it by Jeremy, his last great gift to her. She hated putting herself in danger. She hated constantly being in danger.

She hated all of this so much.

5

T his was not going to be an easy walk. Emily already knew that. But it had been ages since the last time she'd actually gone running, or gone for a hike, and her muscle memory didn't remember what it was like to put in that much effort. As a result, she had barely gotten into the walk when she realized how painful this would be.

She had barely gotten through any of the walk at all.

The distance from Legal to Edmonton was easily twenty-eight miles, maybe thirty. Seemed almost inconsequential when she drove up the highway to get out here. Now, just the prospect of it almost sent her reeling. She was going to have to walk about thirty miles!

And in the middle of the night.

It occurred to Emily how lucky she was that she'd decided not to dress up in order to go investigate and tell off Jeremy. She was angry, she was distraught, and she just wanted to get this over with. So she'd barely changed, with the intent of being comfortable but presentable. She obviously wasn't expecting to be walking down the highway later that evening. If she was, maybe she would've brought a heavier coat, something to keep her warmer.

At the very least, she'd had the good sense to wear running shoes. She would be walking a long time, and she appreciated having some soft soles underneath her feet to keep her going.

She had barely gotten out of the city limits when she realized that her shoes were not going to last forever. They could be the softest choice in the world, she could literally be walking on pillows made of silk, and given the amount of walking she would be doing, plus the fact that she didn't walk all that much—even in her waitressing job, there was more standing involved than actual walking—would result in her getting quite a fair number of blisters tonight.

She tried to avoid thinking of it. Everything else she had to go through tonight—she had lost her boyfriend, her dignity, her stability, possibly her apartment, and her confidence in her daily life—and to top it all off, because of it, because of matters that she did not wish to instigate nor have to live through, she was about to lose a comfortable way to walk.

She was grateful she didn't have to go to her job the next day, but she didn't like the idea of what it was going to be like when she finally did and she could barely stand, let alone walk.

These were all the thoughts running through Emily's head as she finally exited Legal's city limits.

Emily had a long way to go.

Traveling down the road out of the town, she kept her eyes on all the buildings' windows. She didn't see any lights in any of them. It was hard for her to believe that not even one residential household had its lights on late into the evening. No young newlyweds spending the night watching satellite TV. No Goth teenagers hating the fact that they lived in a small rural town, staying up all night as a form of protest.

As best she could figure, Emily determined that in all likelihood, the reason there were no lights on was because most of the people here were probably farmers and would have to get up pretty early to tend to their livelihoods. That, or given the small size and small industry of a place like this, perhaps everybody was elderly. Or possibly everybody else in this town felt the same way she did, and they wanted to spend their evenings going somewhere far more fun, somewhere far livelier.

Lucky them.

One way or another, there were no lights in the surrounding buildings. There was no late night grocery store, no late night pharmacy. It seemed only one bar was necessary to cater to the adult clientele of the town. Anything else that would still be open this late into the night was, in a community this size, possibly something illicit. Which helped Emily decide that she would never even consider going anywhere near a place like that.

A moot point all the same, since there was nowhere else that had its lights on. There was nobody out there to help her.

Emily was on her own.

She had barely left the town. By her estimate, she might have only walked two, maybe three miles at the most. More likely, only one. And it was already cold, and she was tired. She knew that as the night progressed, she would become all the more exhausted, and therefore, her pace would slow down.

And then it would last so, so much longer.

6

A fter several miles of walking, the events that had occurred earlier started to seem like a distant memory to Emily. It was hard to imagine that any of it had happened at all. In truth, the stress she felt from all of the traumatizing experiences she had gone through toward the end of the evening had been both physically and mentally exhausting.

Everything felt like it was so far away.

Perhaps, Emily thought, it might have been simply because of her mind trying to grapple with the sheer distance of the reality in front of her. Maybe, just maybe, the way everything was so far away in real life, it felt more natural to think that her life was so far away as well. But she wasn't adept enough at philosophy or neuroscience to understand whether any of that was true. It was just an entertaining thought.

Considering what she was going through, Emily would need all the entertaining thoughts she could get.

In order to get to Legal, Emily had had to drive down a major highway heading north out of town. She had driven north for several miles before hanging a left and taking a country road a comparatively short distance to reach Legal. All she would have to do in order to get back was take the same route, only in reverse. It seemed easy enough to say it out loud. Though, now that she was in the thick of it, she didn't like the prospect of having to go through it at all.

Firstly, Emily was acutely aware that the travel from Edmonton to the intersection where she had to turn left was the longest portion of the trip to Legal. The rest of the trip after that was only a few miles. Therefore, if she were traveling in reverse, then the trip from the bar in Legal to the intersection where she would now have to turn right would be the quickest and shortest portion of the trip. She knew it would be a good and decent measure of just how much she actually had to walk to get back home.

She was doing everything in her power to conserve the electricity in her cell phone, just in case she managed to get close enough to the city that it would start to work again, so she might be able to call Chandra or even a taxi. However, when she did pull out her phone, she saw that she had wasted at least an hour getting to just this point in the trip. And her feet already hurt, and she was already tired.

It would only be slower going from here on out.

At the very least, there was one thing that was on her mind as she approached the intersection. She was on the major highway heading into the city, which she was certain would drastically increase the rate at which passersby would see her. At first, she was worried that something like this would simply never happen tonight. The entire walk from the town of Legal to the intersection netted a total of zero drivers going past the area. There was nobody there to pick her up. She had started to wonder if it would be like this for the rest of the walk.

Emily was certainly without fault for thinking that way.

What was she expecting? That maybe a trucker would have to make a desperate delivery in the middle of the week and drive through this community? The odds were really against her for anything quite like that happening. In fact, when she'd driven to the bar, she couldn't remember passing that many cars to begin with.

She fully expected that now that she was entering the highway, she would probably get at least one or two cars passing her within the next half hour or so, no matter how unpopulated or late it was.

Which was why she was completely flabbergasted when, looking behind her, the first vehicle that was going to pass by was coming from the very road into Legal that she had just left.

All this walking, and the first car that she had noticed behind her was coming from the place she expected would have zero cars, especially considering the track record she had only just experienced.

She rushed back, frantically waving her arms and calling out as much as she could. This really wasn't a time for decorum or dignity. She just wanted to get back home.

Indeed, it was a truck. And it rumbled up the road.

And in the dead of night, it practically ignored her and turned onto the same intersection she was turning onto. Then it continued on southward, heading into the city.

"Oh, you've got to be fucking kidding me." Emily sighed under her breath. She knew she had no energy to spare on this long hike, but every syllable of that phrase felt like gold. She needed to vent more than anything at this point.

Wallowing in her exhaustion, she knew she had to keep going. Finally, she found the conviction to lift one foot off the ground and keep it moving south. Then the next, followed by the first one, again and again.

She was on the move.

Although this was a major highway, Emily saw that this portion of the road was still fairly far away from any kind of civilization, whether it be a town or another city. It was also, technically, surrounded by farmland. There wasn't any industry here, no commercial zones. Not even a plaza or a gas station. Since most cars traveling through the area would simply be relying on their own high-beams, Emily understood why there were still no streetlights in this area. From a financial standpoint, it wasn't particularly practical.

As a result, the only light she expected to see on the ground would be from cars. Which really weren't there.

Emily began to wonder if she perhaps had heard the distant cries and growls of some wild animal in the night. The thought had crossed her mind on several occasions during the initial portion of the trip. Human civilization had simply pressed into animal territory without a care in the world. So what was one more animal getting encroached on? What was one more animal angry at humans who chased them out of their forest and was willing to look for food closer to the roadway?

Maybe it was because of all the surrounding farmlands. It couldn't be purely agricultural. Surely, some of these farms had animals like cows or chickens. She always heard from her local community market that there were some sweater makers who used local llama fur to make those curiously soft llama fur sweaters. Perhaps there were llama farmers in the area.

But regardless of what kinds of animals were being raised on the surrounding farmland, the point was that there would probably be some wild animal who wished to find a quick snack from them. Possibly a fox or a coyote.

"Wow," Emily said as she considered the possibility of an animal eating her. "Man, that would be a hell of a way to go."

As she continued walking down the highway, another car

drove near her. She saw it long before she ever heard it. It really wasn't that hard, given how dark it was out here. The headlights on the car were practically shining like the sun as they came over the horizon. Emily briefly toyed with the idea of running out into the middle of the highway to flag down the car, probably making the situation more desperate. But she ultimately thought better of it. A driver wouldn't be expecting that, and it was far more likely that he would hit her rather than stop for her. No, Emily decided to stick to the classic hitchhiker methodology of keeping to the side of the road, which was still the safe bet under the circumstances.

She saw the car approaching. Some old hatchback. Emily jumped up and down, waving frantically.

Apparently, the driver didn't even see her, too busy listening to his radio. He drove on past.

"Well, shit," cursed Emily.

Another failure. She turned on her heel and continued to walk southward.

After barely another mile, another serious situation that she had never even considered, though she began to wonder how she was able to ignore it this entire time, hit her like a ton of bricks.

Emily needed to go to the bathroom.

Inevitably, she knew that it would have to happen. She was just amazed that it had to happen out in the middle of nowhere.

In reality, Emily figured she could probably hold it in until she found a rest stop. But then, she wondered why she would even need to bother. Once she had found a rest stop, she would use the opportunity to call for a taxi, regardless of whether she needed to go to the bathroom or otherwise. That, and she remembered the trip up here. There weren't any rest stops for the entire distance.

No, Emily thought, she could probably hold it in, but then

it would be an aggravating pain in her lower stomach, constantly annoying and needling her. Out of everything that had stressed her out this entire evening, she didn't need to add that to her already long list of problems.

It was times like this she wished she were a boy.

Stepping off the highway, she saw she was in an area that wasn't next to any kind of visible farmland, but rather, was next to a forested area. All she would have to do was go a few feet into the tree line, and she would probably have some privacy.

Along the way, she wasn't aware that there was a little gully full of swamp water. She had stepped straight into it, soaking her shoes and socks in the process.

"Well," she murmured, "just one more thing to add to the night, I guess."

Finally getting into the tree line and feeling the squish of the water exiting her shoes with every step, she found an area of the forest she felt was secluded enough that she wouldn't be seen by anybody. Not that there was anybody around to see her, but still.

Pulling down her pants and crouching down, she did everything she could to avoid hitting her shoes and clothes with the stream.

Whatever relief she started to feel was almost immediately interrupted when she saw a car approach and even slow down.

Emily was certain of it. The car was actually slowing down. If she leapt out now, she could probably wave it down and get it to stop completely.

She would probably also wet herself in the process.

She waited rather impatiently. She even tried to contract her legs and maybe even force the stream to come out faster and harder. After a few more seconds, she finished and was able to quickly pull herself together and go leaping out of the trees.

Just in time to see the car speed away.

"Hey!" she cried desperately, chasing after the car and waving her hands in the air. "Stop!"

It was no use. The car had driven on. And all Emily was left with was a sick feeling of having a bunch of bog water squishing around in her shoes as she ran.

This was, by far, the worst night of her life.

After another fifteen or so minutes of walking, Emily could hear a pair of loud bangs in the night sky.

She didn't know what that sound was or what made it. Her immediate thought was that somebody had blown a tire. Since she had just heard two bangs, maybe somebody had blown out two tires. Which wasn't the best thought in the world. Most cars only carried one spare, so whatever car just blew out two tires would be as stranded as she was. Then again, there was always the possibility that the driver had a phone. Perhaps one with a better cell phone provider than hers. Perhaps one that worked.

Maybe, she thought, this night could actually be over sooner than she expected.

7

"See, the real problem is that there's no such thing as a prenuptial agreement for relationships that aren't nuptial. So if you can't go into a boyfriend-girlfriend relationship without some kind of contractual obligation to each other, then you're shooting yourself in the foot by making a serious commitment. A marriage contract is the easiest way to ensure that you still get to keep your stuff if everything goes to shit. I mean, boyfriends and girlfriends can't do that. Someone's going to lose the apartment. And it's not like I can really go to court over keeping my apartment now that we're broken up. I can barely buy vegetables, let alone pay a lawyer."

Emily had been talking to herself since she started walking. But by this point, her 'talking to herself' episodes had become full-blown conversations.

Which, when she started thinking about it, made a certain amount of sense. She was stuck out in the rural countryside, in the middle of the night. She was walking an endless southern road, with no twists and turns, for hours now. The horizon never got closer, and the view never got clearer. It was almost easy to trick herself into thinking she wasn't making any progress at all.

Which was a thought that she didn't appreciate, given that her feet certainly felt the pain.

And so, in order to take her mind off the pain, the drudgery, and the loneliness, she needed a distraction. And talking to herself was just as easily a distraction as anything else.

"Sometimes, it's not really about any kind of formal sense and sensibility," she continued, "but it's about filling dead air space. After all, we're very social creatures. We want to get along. We want to interact with each other. This is why when we're alone, we want to be able to make it seem as if we are a part of something, filling the gap that should normally be filled with another voice or another friend. Basically, the same reason we turn on the radio whenever we're in the car. Weird how that became a societal norm, but when you talk to yourself while walking down the street, all of a sudden, you're crazy. I blame the Victorian era. The human race did a lot of stuff that was considered perfectly normal before the Victorians came along, and then a bunch of scared upper-class traumatized British middle-aged virgins swooped in and decided to ruin it for everybody."

Emily looked up and suddenly stopped talking.

Up ahead, there appeared to be flashing lights. They were still pretty faded and distant, but they were distinct. And red.

And they weren't increasing or decreasing in luminosity. Which meant that they were a stable source.

Possibly a parked car.

Emily started to shake and grabbed her face in her hands. She didn't want to get her hopes up since those lights could mean anything—maybe they were even a mirage, given her exhausted state—but she was already feeling an adrenaline surge, like she had been granted an incredible amount of power and energy at the sight of this great new hope.

She wanted to believe that there was really a car there. She wanted to believe that it would all soon be over.

Ignoring the pain in the soles of her feet, she started running down the road as best she could without increasing her exhaustion and slowing down again, which ultimately meant that she barely hobbled toward the lights. It didn't matter to her. As long as those lights were getting closer, she would run and enjoy every moment of the experience.

First, she watched as the lights got bright enough that beams could be seen distinctly in the night sky.

Then she could make out the shape of the lights. They were definitely the rear lights of a car.

It was unmistakable now. There was definitely a car parked up the road. And now, she was going to get to it, and she was going to figure out what to do from there.

Maybe they had a working phone. Maybe they could give her a ride into town. Maybe, even if they were stuck on the side of the road for some reason, they would still have a means of getting help. Maybe they were traveling with friends who were going to get help, or somebody was expecting them and would come looking for them. But in any scenario, the result was the same. She was going to find somebody, and they were going to have the power and the capability to get her home, to put an end to this horrible, horrible night for her.

Before she would have to wake up the next morning and deal with another horrible day.

Emily was fully aware of that with every step that she ran toward the car. But with her whole body sweating into every bit of clothing she was wearing, with her shoes doing nothing to protect her feet at this point, with her face dry and aching from the tears she barely even noticed, the problems of tomorrow seemed like an issue a long way off. All she cared about now was to simply be rescued.

Somebody to take her far, far away from Jeremy and his new whore.

As she started to get closer, she could see why the lights appear to be flashing on the back of the car. whoever was parked there was flashing the emergency lights. Okay, a concerning setback, but not a debilitating one. Maybe they had a burst tire and were simply replacing it with their emergency tire. Maybe they just needed to check directions on the side of the road and had parked there for purely innocent reasons. The fact that they were attracting attention to themselves with these lights indicated to Emily that they weren't—fingers crossed—lovers off to the side of the road. It was a long shot that anything like that would happen, but at the same time, Emily didn't want to ruin these people's evening. It would make for an awkward rescue.

After several minutes of running, Emily passed by the first road sign she'd seen in quite some time. It was a green highway sign, indicating that the town of Morinville was off to the right. A few yards beyond that, she had to cross the intersection with a perpendicular highway. Vaguely being able to picture the way on a map, she knew that she had almost reached the halfway point between where she was and where she was going. As for the car, it was just up ahead, and hopefully, it would be able to drive for the rest of the way.

As she finally got closer, she saw that it was a reasonably modern car. It was also a shade of blue, same as Jeremy's.

When she got even closer, she saw that it was even shaped like Jeremy's.

In fact, it was the exact make and model of Jeremy's car.

At this distance, and with the flashing emergency lights blaring in her eyes, she still couldn't read the license plate in the darkness of night. Still, though, she started wondering if maybe it was Jeremy's car.

What were the odds that Jeremy and his new girlfriend— his new slut—ended up getting into a car accident on the way back home, the same night they broke up?

"No," she whispered. "No way. It couldn't be!"

Once she was upon the car, she could see very clearly that the license plate matched Jeremy's. And everything was exactly the way she saw it every day when they used his car.

It really was a car crash. This was actually Jeremy's car!

But did they go off to find help? Together? She wondered why they would be so stupid as to not leave at least one of them behind.

She glimpsed into the car, and she saw both Jeremy and that new girl . . . Erica, Emily vaguely remembered.

And they were both dead.

8

Emily fell backward and crawled on her hands and feet, crab walking as fast as she could away from the car.

She covered her face, struggling not to see anything, desperate to try to get the image out of her head. But she couldn't stop seeing the two faces with bloody gashes and the pools of blood on the dash and the windshield. She couldn't erase the image of Jeremy facing an awkward direction as a portion of his neck was sticking out away from the bottom of his head.

Something horrible had happened.

There was no movement from the front of the car. There was no noise coming from there, either. These two people were definitely dead.

Jeremy had been her boyfriend earlier that afternoon. They'd broken up very dramatically. The last time she saw him, he was brushing her off like she didn't matter. He was going to spend the rest of his life mocking her with his new slutty little college girl.

And now he was dead.

Emily processed the thought. She didn't know how to feel about that. She was so frustrated with him, so angry with him. But she wondered if she was supposed to be feeling happy at the prospect of his actually being dead.

She sincerely hoped she would never feel happy about it. If anything, she only felt revulsion at the sight of it.

It was so horrible, so disgusting. They had been mutilated. How could they have died in a car crash?

Breathing heavily and trying to stomach the thought of what she had just witnessed, Emily stood up and attempted to rationalize the situation. It was still pretty difficult to contemplate. After all, she had seen these two people alive and well maybe two or three hours ago.

She felt as if she'd been walking for days, talking to herself along the highway for so long, she'd lost track of time. She wasn't even sure what time she'd actually left Legal. She wasn't sure how long she'd been walking, really. After a while, it didn't matter.

Right now, in particular. She was standing a fair distance from a car that currently contained the dead bodies of her ex-boyfriend and his lover. Earlier that night, they had basically ruined her life.

She still didn't know what any of this meant.

What had happened here? Emily studied the car from her vantage point. She didn't want to get any closer.

Its wheels were undamaged. And yes, a part of the car was leaning off the highway into the ditch, but it hadn't gone fully into the ditch. Realistically, it could've been driven out again. It certainly didn't flip over.

The windshield was intact. Even though there was blood all over it, Emily could see it wasn't even cracked, or at least, not more so than she remembered. If they didn't crash through the windshield, then why were they so mutilated?

There wasn't any damage to the front of the car, not large

enough to indicate a crash. Now that she looked more closely, there appeared to be a dent in the driver's side door. She didn't remember a dent there before.

It almost looked as if they had suffered a collision from the side. But what kind? They didn't crash into anything. They didn't flip over. If they'd knocked into something, then where was the other thing they knocked into? There was nothing else on the road, and if they had hit another car, there would've been some evidence of that. By all accounts, it seemed as if something had hit the car from the side.

But otherwise, the car had sustained such little damage that it shouldn't have been able to kill anybody driving in it, certainly not two people. Injure, maybe, perhaps in the form of a bash on the head or a sprained wrist.

There was nothing there to explain how two people could be slashed into pieces, having their faces mutilated, their eyes gouged out. They didn't crash in any way that would do that to them.

By all initial indications of what had happened to the car, Emily figured that they would've been able to easily drive back onto the road. The car was in good condition, still drivable. So if the dent in the door was any indication, they had been forced off the road and then killed. By some means other than a car crash. Something had happened to them.

Something had done this.

Was it a wild animal? Emily thought that made sense, except there weren't any scratches on the outside of the car. There was no animal in the car, and she didn't see any droppings or fur. So if it was some animal, then it was an animal that had swooped in and left without really gaining anything or leaving anything behind.

Emily didn't consider herself any kind of forensics expert or anything. She thought she could take a closer look at the bodies and see if they had any bite marks on them. Except, that would mean having to look at the bodies again, obviously.

She had only barely started to block out the image of her dead ex-boyfriend in the driver's seat. She didn't want to see it again.

Only problem was, every single car that had passed by her was not willing to stop and pick her up. Also, at this late hour, even though there were more cars here than on the road to Legal, it still wasn't much of an increase. And she still had quite a lot of walking to do.

There was always the possibility that Jeremy had his phone on him and that he hadn't changed his password to access it.

She didn't contemplate the idea of searching through Erica's things because she didn't know her and wouldn't know what to do if she had even found a phone of hers. Briefly, the thought entered her mind of maybe moving the bodies and using the car herself to drive back home. But considering all the trouble she'd gotten into back at the bar, she didn't want to compound that with the idea of disturbing a crime scene by moving corpses.

At this point, the wisest decision she could make was to simply try to track down Jeremy's phone. Maybe it would work.

Maybe she could do it without throwing up.

As she gingerly approached the driver's side door, the smell of blood started to permeate everything, and the aroma of the air was rich with iron. Emily had tasted it in her own mouth at different times in her life, but there was something truly disgusting about feeling it in her nostrils when the blood wasn't hers. Something about that seemed very grotesque, very putrid. On the bright side, it made her want to close her eyes as she approached. She didn't want to see what she already knew was there. She didn't want to be reminded.

But she also knew she wouldn't be able to do this blindly. She had to steady herself. She could already feel her fist shaking.

Crouching down next to the door, she leaned up and slowly opened it, using the cuff of her sleeve to keep from leaving fingerprints. She knew she shouldn't be messing with a crime scene, but she felt she had no other choice. She needed that phone.

She refused to look at the bodies, but as the door opened, she could see its driver's side interior. There was blood, yes, but also it looked like some biomatter. Maybe skin. Maybe some organ, like brains.

Emily started shaking and desperately glanced away, staring at the sky instead.

Suppressing her gag reflex and trying to imagine that the iron smell was anything other than blood, she slowly reached her covered hand in around the frame of the car door and tried to find Jeremy's jacket. From there, she figured she would be able to move her hand across his body—she tried not to think of the words 'his dead body'—and find his pants, where he probably kept his phone in his pocket. Probably. Hopefully.

The truth was, she wasn't actually sure where he kept his phone. Maybe he kept it in his back pocket. For all she knew, he kept it in the glove compartment. It seemed she didn't know Jeremy as well as she'd thought.

She wasn't sure when the last time they'd even had sex was. Or had a decent conversation.

She just kept telling herself that relationships had down-times, and that was just how things went. It wasn't really evidence of anything falling apart.

Until this afternoon, when it clearly was.

Breathing in deeply, Emily snapped back to reality when the scent of blood filled her lungs again. Somehow, her mind had wandered back to their old relationship. She understood why, of course. She wanted to think of better things and better times, anywhere but here, anything but today. But this really wasn't the time for being nostalgic. She had to deal with this disgusting work first.

She reminded herself that she had to focus on the last thing she wanted to be doing at the moment, which was finding his phone.

She reached out across his body and found his jacket. A simple shake revealed that there was nothing in the pockets. "Dammit," she muttered.

She'd have to touch his body. To do that, she needed to look at it. She shivered but then forced herself to focus. There was no way she wasn't going to get blood on her if she had to touch him. She'd have to try to keep it to a minimum. She shifted her position and leaned in over the body, scanning his button-down shirt, which she could now see was entirely soaked with blood.

She reached out, ready to check his shirt pocket first, but then as her hand touched his chest near the pocket, she noticed there were jagged tears in the fabric of the shirt.

The injuries weren't just to their faces. Jeremy's stomach was slashed open.

A long slash. Not with claws or teeth. This could only have been done with a knife.

A person did this!

Emily froze again. *Who could've done this? And why?*

Questions for later. She shivered as she shoved those thoughts away. She moved her hand down the bloody shirt until she reached Jeremy's familiar belt buckle. She moved her hand closer along the belt line until she reached his pants' front pocket, which was mercifully not that drenched with blood. She reached in.

Some loose change. And his wallet. Nothing more.

"Of course, Jeremy would keep his cell phone on his right side," Emily said, cursing under her breath.

Well, she thought, taking a deep gulp, *nothing for it but to just do it.*

She reached her hand across his stomach and glided it toward the right pocket, leaning farther into the car to be able to reach. She tried to look away, but as she moved, she saw the open slit in Jeremy's stomach, revealing his intestines, and gagged.

Her head shook, and her nose flared. Emily tried to close her eyes, but she still remembered what it looked like even when they were shut tight.

She gave a high-pitched squeal as she dipped her hand into his right pocket. This pocket was heavily stained. She could feel her fingers digging through sticky, glue-like liquid. Coagulating blood.

Mercifully, she also felt his phone.

She pulled it out of his pocket, and in pushing herself away, she unfortunately pushed herself off Jeremy's body, unintentionally using it for leverage, and flung herself to the dirty asphalt. She crawled away rapidly. Looking down, her hand was a dark red, dripping with Jeremy's blood as if she had just driven her hand straight into his body cavity. His phone was also drenched, dripping with blood.

Ignoring the horror of what she'd seen in the car, she looked down at her arm and saw stains of his blood all over her arm. Looking further, she noticed her jacket and her pants were also stained with bits of blood and what looked like bits of skin. For all she knew, maybe they were.

Briefly tolerating the idea of being horribly disgusted by having all this on her, she realized what this would probably look like to any police officers who might come by. She didn't want to throw away all her clothes and walk down the side of the highway naked, but she certainly didn't want to walk around still smelling all this blood on her.

As a last resort, Emily headed toward the ditch and began to wipe her arm off on the grass, trying to get as much of the blood and gross stuff off her as possible. Unfortunately, a lot of it still stuck to her clothing, staining it.

She turned the phone on. It still worked, even though the screen was covered in blood. She punched in the pass code, which thankfully, also worked.

And there was no service. No Wi-Fi, no cellular. Nothing at all.

Which seemed odd to Emily. She had hoped that it was just her phone that had dropped the service. But if it was Jeremy's phone as well . . . if it really was all phones . . . then what happened to the service? She had just passed by a road sign indicating that there was another town two miles to the west. Wouldn't they have some sort of cell service tower? Emily knew she was in a rural area, but it couldn't have been quite so primitive, could it? Her phone had worked fine on the way to Legal, so it couldn't be that there were no towers.

All the same, it seemed as if it was an entirely wasted experience. After all that, she still didn't have a working phone. Disgusted by what she'd had to go through, she refused to consider the possibility of trying to get into Jeremy's car and driving away that way.

She would just have to accept the situation and walk on.

After only about ten feet, Emily had gotten to a place where she could forget about the slowly drying blood on her clothes. She picked up her pace with a new sense of vigor, desperate to get home.

A moment later, Emily heard an engine and wheels rolling on the pavement approaching from behind her.

She hadn't heard a car approaching, and suddenly, one was coming up right next to her. She must've been seriously distraught by the dead bodies to not even notice.

The car came to a halt next to her as she started to slow down. She backed away, worried about what the driver would think when he saw her covered in blood. She ran through excuses in her head, figuring she would tell the driver what had happened. When she quickly ran the situation through her mind, however, she realized how preposterous and suspicious it all sounded, and how if she were in the driver's shoes, she wouldn't really be that trusting of somebody walking down the highway drenched in blood.

But Emily also knew she was desperate enough to try. At this point, even if the driver called the police on her, at least she would get home.

She looked inside the car and saw a familiar face.

It had been such a horrible evening, with so many terrible things happening to her, but still, even after everything she'd been through, she certainly wouldn't forget the nerdy-looking middle-aged guy who tried to pick her up at the bar after she broke up with Jeremy.

"Hey there," he called out, smiling. "Hope you're still doing all right. I think we got off on the wrong foot. Let me properly introduce myself. I'm Daniel. What's your name?"

Emily stared and could feel her spine getting cold. Did he not see the blood covering her? Or was he talking like this while being fully aware of it? She wasn't sure which was worse.

"W-what?" Emily stammered. "What are you doing here?"

"The fuck it looks like I'm doing here? I'm offering a ride. Now do you want to get in or not?"

Something's wrong, Emily thought. She was covered in blood. The car crash with Jeremy's and Erica's bodies was still visible thirty feet behind them. This creepy guy just happened to be here in his sedan, and he was acting as if none of this was an issue.

Emily turned on her heel and kept walking on the highway. There was no way that this was going to be the only car that would pull over for her. She refused to believe it.

"Look," he said more forcefully. "You can either get in the car, or you can keep walking for freaking ever."

Emily ignored him. She walked away faster.

"Okay, fine," he said, leaning out the window. "Good fucking luck on the road, you stupid bitch."

He suddenly revved his engine. It startled Emily.

"See," he yelled further, "this is why you were dumped. You keep going for stupid assholes, and when a nice guy like me tries to do the right thing, you think you're too good for me. You don't know how to see a good thing when it's right in your fucking face."

She barely heard the last part as he drove off and raced away into the night.

It wasn't the first time she'd had to deal with some asshole yelling obscenities at her in her life. But she was very aware that it was the first time that it was in the middle of a dark highway. And she was completely alone.

At best, Daniel was a misogynistic asshole. But more likely, he was an extremely dangerous individual who hated her.

And he was the only person who'd stopped to talk to her this entire night.

9

"Well, on the plus side," Emily said out loud, "at least this part of the ditch didn't have any bog water in it."

It was, by any measure, a delayed reaction. Even Emily knew that it would've been the right thing to say about fifteen minutes, maybe a half hour, ago. That said, it was something soothing to say and something soothing to hear. Quite a lot had happened, and even this symbolic pat on the back was something she had to do in order to cheer herself up.

The reason she was happy that this portion of the ditch didn't have any bog water was because the last time she'd crossed the ditch that separated the highway from the nearby countryside, it happened to be filled with a lot of water, almost turning it into a small filthy pond. She had pretty much destroyed her sneakers and socks, possibly risked infecting her feet, in crossing through that shit. Since then, she had almost entirely forgotten about it. Particularly since, not long after that time, she'd ended up sticking her arm into a mutilated corpse and coating herself with their blood.

Comparatively speaking, the dampness on her shoes just didn't really seem to measure up anymore.

That said, she was grateful that she didn't have to go through it again when crossing the ditch a second time. This time, however, her reason for going into the nearby forest next to the highway wasn't to answer the call of nature.

Rather, it was to put a barrier between herself and Daniel.

Ever since their encounter, she'd been completely unnerved by the entire experience. There was so much wrong with it, and the more she thought about it, the more she realized that everything about it was wrong, and it only escalated with each examination.

Firstly, there was the surface terror of it all—being confronted by a creepy guy on the highway who'd deliberately pulled over just to yell obscenities at her would put anybody off. He was a disgusting little troll, and she didn't even want to risk the possibility that he would circle around and try to pick her up again or, even worse, assault her. At the very least, now that she had a large ditch between her and the highway, Daniel would probably have enough common sense not to try to drive up to her, knowing he would fall in. Or if he didn't, he would crash his car into the ditch, and well, Emily wouldn't lose any sleep over that. Anything that would keep him away. She supposed there was always a possibility that he might actually get out of his car and try to run after her over the ditch, but that would be a pretty serious escalation of tonight's situation. She was hoping it wouldn't come to that.

She'd never even considered searching Jeremy's car for a potential weapon that she could use against Daniel.

Which brought Emily to her second thought, the very real risk that Daniel was somehow involved in the deaths of Jeremy and Erica.

Emily really couldn't get her mind off the idea, the more she tried to wrap her head around it. After all, Daniel had slowed down and approached her to pick her up while Jeremy's car was still in sight. Daniel didn't make any mention of it. He didn't ask her if her car needed some work or if he needed to call the tow service. And at that proximity, it was very likely that Daniel would've been able to see the damage to the driver's side door and, likely, the bloody windshield. And even if he'd somehow missed all of those details, it was hard to imagine that his lustful eyes wouldn't have been able to notice that Emily was drenched in blood.

Frankly, it was impossible to consider the idea that Daniel hadn't noticed something was up with the car, with the entire bloody scene. And he'd never mentioned it. Like he didn't notice or didn't care.

Or possibly, Emily thought, because he was already aware of it.

Another point to consider was the fact that he just seemed to have come out of nowhere. It was a long and empty highway in the middle of the night. In the few instances whenever a vehicle drove down the road, Emily could hear it already coming over the horizon, and she was fully prepared to flag it down and try to get them to stop, to give her a ride. Back before she was drenched in blood, of course.

But not Daniel's car. No sir, not Daniel's car. It seemed to have appeared behind her, and it had its engine turned off as it inched closer. It was like the whole trip was planned. She certainly would've been able to hear it if it was coming down the main highway. He couldn't have possibly coasted down the highway from that distance on a neutral engine for that long and maintained any kind of speed in his approach toward her. That was ridiculous.

Emily rubbed her chin, pondering the situation. So if he didn't come down from the highway . . .

Then he must have been coming in from around the

intersection Emily had passed by before seeing Jeremy's car. The one that led toward Morinville. It was the only conceivable way Emily could picture his car suddenly showing up, if it was able to come around from a different direction, having all that noise blocked out by the surrounding trees, farming fenceposts, and road signs.

But if that was the case, Emily thought further, then what was he even doing there? Because that was another important issue. Where was he before this? After all, the only reason she even recognized him was because she'd seen him earlier that evening at the bar.

In Legal.

Which didn't really make a lot of sense. Daniel clearly had a car, and Emily didn't. If he had left shortly after her— hell, if he had left long after her—then in the car, he would've been able to pass her by far sooner and already be on his way south toward Edmonton. Obviously, there was a very real possibility that he had only recently left the bar and had spent the night after his rejection sitting around the bar, or maybe going out to do whatever, before passing by on the main highway. That was the only realistic explanation for why it took him this long to suddenly show up next to her. If he had left any earlier, he would've been long gone by now.

But if her theory about Daniel sneaking up on her from a side road was right . . . then she realized that the only way he could've come out of that side road was if he was coming from Morinville.

A completely different town, south of Legal. Both of them off the highway.

And yes, granted, there were back roads all over the place that could be used to get from one township to another. But why would any driver willingly choose to head south this way? If Daniel really was heading south toward Edmonton, he would've used the highway. He would have no reason to head south from Legal to Morinville, then turn and head toward the main highway, just to go to Edmonton . . . past her.

Emily's body went cold. Everything sounded damn suspicious, but now it was starting to sound pretty creepy as well. Strictly speaking, the only way such a route could've possibly made any sense would be if Daniel had a very specific reason to be in that little side street, the one heading toward Morinville.

And the only answer she could picture why he would want to go in that direction, when he was supposedly heading south, was because it was a quiet place to wait for her.

Her mind raced as she considered other possibilities. Perhaps he had gone down the highway too far, and he simply turned onto the side road toward Morinville, and then . . . waited there until he could leave just as she showed up?

She knew what that sounded like. Paranoid. Borderline crazy. But there wasn't a sensible way to rationalize why he'd suddenly appeared next to her, other than sheer coincidence. Which, admittedly, would've been a reasonable explanation if not for the fact that he seemed so calm as he was passing Jeremy's car and talking to a woman drenched in blood. If he really was just heading home to Edmonton, circumstantially passing her at that precise moment, then wouldn't a normal person be surprised by what he saw?

But not Daniel, Emily thought. *No, definitely not Daniel.*

Not the guy who'd tried to pick her up at a bar. Not the guy who'd reacted so violently to being rejected. Not the guy who'd acted so monstrously when turned away on the highway. Not the guy who, every time he ever presented himself, gave off the feeling that he didn't want her to see who he really was.

Not the guy with a damaged car hood.

Emily was starting to pick up all the other little details that, the more she thought of them, the less paranoid they sounded. When Daniel had passed her by, she had been terrified to see him, but she seemed to vaguely recall that the front of his car had some damage to the hood and on the right side. The kind of damage she would expect if the right side of his car had suffered a collision.

Maybe if it had driven into another car.

Also, Jeremy and Erica had been alive several hours ago. The corpses were fresh. They had died very recently. And very recently, as in just before she had stumbled upon them farther down the highway. She recalled that she had heard some loud bangs. At first, she'd thought it was tires bursting. She thought that was why she saw a car on the side of the road.

But Jeremy's wheels were fine. And he had certainly lost a lot of blood. And bits of his brains and innards were seen around different parts of the car, like by the door and on the windshield.

Almost as if part of his body had been blown out. Maybe by a gunshot or two.

Emily had to stop and take a deep breath.

The more she kept repeating these words in her own mind, and the more she occasionally said them out loud, the more insane they sounded. The more they felt like the ramblings of a paranoid lunatic.

Emily was exhausted. Walking in the ditch wasn't as quick as walking on the edge of the highway. It was more tiring as well. It would take her forever to get back to Edmonton walking this way.

All the same, she was completely willing to do it. No matter what was going on with Daniel, no matter what was actually going on with this whole situation, Emily was absolutely certain of one thing—Daniel was a creepy little fuck.

And anything she could do to put some distance between herself and the highway where she knew he was lurking was a good idea in her book.

10

I t had been a very long time since Emily had last checked her phone. Earlier in the evening, she had checked it frequently to see if there was a possibility that she was within range of a cell tower and could get an adequate signal that would allow her to make a call.

She quickly realized that the more she checked, the more battery power she ended up using with each check. It didn't seem like a lot at first, but becoming frustrated at not having access to her phone, she kept doing it to the point where it started to seem as if she was draining the power out of her phone with incredible speed. She didn't want to risk the possibility of losing the use of her phone by the time she actually got to an area where she was certain her cell service would return, when she finally got back to the city limits of Edmonton. She needed to preserve her battery for that, at least.

As such, she didn't even know what time it was. By this point, it must surely be long after midnight. Maybe it was even one or two in the morning. And here she was, stuck out in the middle of nowhere.

She wondered what she would have to answer for once she actually got back into town. Surely, the first rational person she ran into would be horrified by the fact that she had dried blood on her clothes. Even if she didn't request to be taken to a police station, she would likely get rounded up immediately anyway. Then she would have to explain how she'd found her ex-boyfriend and his lover dead in his car by the highway. How she'd decided to see if they had a phone that worked and contaminated the crime scene. She would have to acknowledge that yes, it was very suspicious that they both died shortly after she specifically drove out to meet them and commenced an altercation with them, an altercation that—oh, right, she was almost able to forget about that —an altercation that had resulted in her hitting a bartender. So assault on top of all that.

And now that she thought about it a little further, the only reason she knew that Jeremy and Erica were having an affair in the first place was because of the mysterious note that had been left underneath her door. One that she didn't have with her anymore because she'd thrown it at Jeremy in the bar, and if the police asked her about it, she wouldn't be able to tell them where she got it, who gave it to her, or where it was now because she simply had no idea.

Emily almost started to laugh through her tears. If the police decided to declare her legally insane for following a mysterious note that might have just been a figment of her imagination, they could just source the fact that she had been running around in the middle of the night covered in blood from the corpse of her ex-boyfriend a few hours after she'd jealously confronted him.

Somehow, Emily managed to convince herself that things were going to be a lot harder when Jeremy was still alive. But that seemed like so long ago now.

Emily took a moment to look up. She noticed the sky was

full of stars, glistening brilliant and white, the way they were always depicted in television movies, designed to make you feel good. The kind of night sky city people rarely saw anymore with all the light pollution. The kind of sky that Emily figured human beings didn't deserve anymore. The kind that was so majestic and so rich with nature that it almost made a person feel small. It was very humbling.

The sublime experience she felt staring up at the sky was almost immediately ruined when she heard a car engine rev on the opposite side of the highway.

It was him again. Daniel.

"Yoo-hoo," he called out, sticking his head out the driver's side window and waving in her direction. "I know you're there. I can see you."

Emily ignored him. She walked on.

"Bitch," he called out into the night. "Bitch . . ." And then he drove away, heading north this time. Emily was certain that he was smiling.

After all, he'd smiled every other time.

Emily knew there was something seriously wrong with Daniel. So the creepy guy who'd tried to pick her up at the bar had apparently decided to try to pick her up again, get her into his car, and when he failed, just yell at her horrendously before driving off. All of that was disturbing enough, but Emily was fully expecting that most guys would simply drive off and call it a night after that. But not Daniel. Definitely not Daniel.

Her reprieve from him was short-lived, as after about ten minutes, he returned, coming back from the north, where he once again slowed down.

This time, he didn't bother to ask her if she wanted a ride. He just started yelling obscenities at her and made some obscene comments about her body; then he drove off again.

Emily was certain that this man was insane. He was deliberately going out of his way to circle around on the highway just so he could show up next to her again and yell at her. He was doing it just to haunt her. Just to harass her.

He never yelled anything that was clever or developmentally impressive. He always had a high-pitched sneer that made him sound infantile, though he was exercising a lot of power. And he kept doing it over and over. He could've left a long time ago. He could've called the police. He was the one with the car. He obviously had the power to do so.

This is almost worse than if he were a rapist or a murderer, she briefly thought. Because if he was, then he would've already taken advantage of her a long time ago. He was the one with the car and had the size and weight advantage over her. He would be able to do anything.

But he never left the car. Not even once. And the most that he did that could be called a 'difference' was to variate what it was that he was yelling at her. Sometimes he yelled that she was a 'damn whore' and a 'fucking slut'. Sometimes he pretended to be her while yelling, "Oh, look at me. I think I'm better than everybody else." And sometimes—as evidenced with his most recent passing—he would simply try to be annoying. Maybe gently calling out some insult to her in a whiny, slow, nasally tone.

Nothing was accomplished by any of it, as far as Emily was concerned. He simply had the power to do so. And she couldn't do a damn thing to stop him.

There were very few cars on the road, but one did pass. Regrettably, she made no effort to try to wave it down. She wouldn't have dared. There was always the risk that if she tried, Daniel could show up out of nowhere. So now, because of him, Emily was missing the possibility of hitchhiking her way back home.

He was deliberately making this experience more miserable for her. He was deliberately going out of his way to hurt her.

And why? Because she'd turned him down in a bar?

Yes, this guy was crazy. She hated him with every fiber of her being.

She heard the wheels rolling and slowing down. By this point, it had become rather familiar. And lo and behold, Daniel's sedan slowed down by the side of the road, heading south this time, as he leaned out the window.

Only this time, he didn't even yell anything discernible. He was just making horrible noises. It almost sounded like a donkey braying. Or some sort of horse or mule.

This was a grown man. A middle-aged man was spending the late hours of the evening going out of his way to do this.

Emily finally stopped and turned on her heel. "What the fuck is wrong with you? Why can't you just piss off?"

Daniel made the braying sound once more. "That's what you sound like when you talk."

Emily knew that ignoring him wouldn't make a difference, but she couldn't think of anything else to do. After all, she still had to get home somehow. So she continued to walk on, grateful there was at least a ditch between them.

He slowly drove down the highway, braying like a mule for what seemed like a good two or three minutes, until he finally yelled, "Listen to me when I talk to you!" And then he drove off again.

On several occasions, Emily had wondered what would happen to her if she made a sharp turn and ran into the forest that was along the highway. She decided against it for several reasons. Firstly, this land was either private property —which would put her at the mercy of any hunting traps or men with rifles she came across, as well as add to her increasing list of committed crimes tonight—or it was wild government property, so it was allowed to act as a nature preserve. Meaning, for the most part, that these woods were probably infested with wolves and coyotes. She was almost certain that when looking into the darkness of the forest, she could spot a pair of glowing eyes staring back at her.

Although at this point, she wasn't sure if that was actually the sighting of an animal or just her paranoia taking over. She didn't know which would be worse, being mauled by a creature in the forest or being harmed by Daniel. She didn't know which of them was the wilder animal.

To her left was the occasional respite on a highway that was now dominated by some disturbing freak who wouldn't let her go. To her right was potential death in the middle of the night in the wild lands of the rural countryside. And above her was a star-filled night sky, reminding her of earlier times when she could stop and think and dream about innocent things. Times when she wasn't lost out in the darkness, with no way of reaching the outside world and no way of knowing if something was going to harm her or kill her from any direction.

How much more of her life was going to be taken from her without her consent?

The muscles in her calves and her thighs burned as if they were doused in hot gasoline. Every joint she had ached with pain. At this point, the only way Emily was able to continue moving her legs was by lifting each one off the ground and hoisting and throwing it, practically as if she were swinging a wrecking ball. And it was all made harder by the fact that she was trudging across uneven ground.

She was hungry, she was depressed, and she was exhausted. She just wanted to go home. And she knew that at the rate she was walking, she would probably never get there at a reasonable time.

But as if the universe were trying to send a signal, the ditch grew shallower. The uneven path she was using to walk eventually narrowed toward the highway and drew her closer to the paved road. After another minute or two of walking, the ground leveled out, and the forest to her right encroached on her walking space, pushing her closer to the road.

Evidently, whatever engineers worked on this portion of the highway seemed to agree that the trees encroaching on the area were a potential hazard because here, they'd decided to install a metal barrier, which would likely keep a car from driving directly into the trees should it skid off the road or if some fatigued driver lost control of his wheel. In any case, Emily did appreciate seeing the barrier there. It made her feel as though some progress was being made. She wasn't just wasting her time. She was slowly getting back to her home city.

Not even thinking about the circumstances she was going through at the moment, she immediately leapt over the metal barrier—as much as possible, as her legs were exhausted, and her leap was more like an uncomfortable overstep—and continued to walk down the asphalt.

In some ways, it was like a weight had been lifted from her shoulders, one that Emily didn't even know was there until it was gone. After a step or two, the excess dirt stuck to the bottom of her shoes began to scrape off. Another two steps, and the soles of her shoes could grip the road once more, and with each subsequent step, she could feel herself pushing forward, making strides and distance. The movements were easier on her exhausted muscles, and she didn't feel like she was putting in half of her energy just to balance her weight on shaky soil. She felt like she could actually face forward.

How much time and energy had she wasted walking through unstable dirt? How much of the night had been spent struggling to continue through terrain that only made it far more difficult for her and, ironically enough, far more dangerous? Because after all, Emily's whole reason for walking on the dirt path across the ditch by the highway was to keep away from the actual roadway so that if Daniel were driving by, he would never be able to get too close. But by doing so, she had slowed her pace to such an extent that she was staying out here far longer than intended and, therefore, spending more time being hounded by this idiot in his sedan. She should've just stayed on the asphalt the entire time, she realized.

Now she practically marched with dedicated energy, moving forward in a way she never could've imagined. She faced forward, flinging her arms back and forth, filling herself with adrenaline, powered by optimism and enthusiasm, in a way she hadn't been since before she got that note slipped under her door in her apartment. And maybe, just maybe, if she kept her pace and her energy, she would be back at her apartment soon enough.

It took Emily a moment to realize that focusing so much of her energy on moving forward and listening to the sound of her voice with such enthusiastic notes about how well she was suddenly doing, she had stopped paying attention to any vehicles on the road.

And once she had started paying attention again, she couldn't help but notice the sound she dreaded.

A car engine revving. Very loudly.

And what was worse, steadily and almost rhythmically.

Emily already knew it was going to be Daniel. She obviously didn't want it to be Daniel, but seriously, who else could it have possibly been?

The asphalt directly in front of her began to illuminate rather quickly.

When she turned to look, she could see that the car was now driving very, very rapidly, with its high beams on, blasting massively powerful lights all the way down the highway, all the way until the horizon. It was as if the car was ready to destroy anything it rode toward, or even the earth underneath its wheels.

And when Emily figured that she was close enough to have been seen distinctly by its driver, the car suddenly made a heavy turn and veered straight toward the metal barrier.

Daniel was steering the car directly toward her.

11

With a gasp, Emily leapt back and dove toward the metal barrier, then rushed toward the trees, pressing herself against one tightly. The sedan, having plowed over where she had just been standing a moment ago, ended up barely missing her. Instead of a head-on collision with her, the car sped with maximum force past her and careened off the metal barrier barely a few feet in front of her.

In the rush of the situation, Emily managed to move forward again and glance at the front of the car after it collided with the barrier. It was hard to discern, since it was all happening so fast, and she certainly couldn't deny that she had just witnessed a car crash into a large metal object. That said, despite all these factors, Emily was fully convinced that she could see damage on the front of the car, toward the right side. She hadn't imagined it.

It was precisely where she would expect the damage to be if this car had rammed another car from the driver's side.

It wasn't conclusive evidence. And now, since Daniel had damaged his car even further, it would probably be difficult for even the most expert forensics detective to be able to discern one set of damage from another, especially since they were both so close to each other in the same evening. But in Emily's mind, she had confirmed her fears. This car had definitely received damage on its right side from colliding with another object.

Against Jeremy's door, more than likely.

As far as she was concerned, Daniel had rammed his car off the side of the road into them and then blasted them with a pair of bullets. And then, for whatever insane reason he devised in his sick head, he'd also torn them apart with a knife.

And now, after several hours of harassing and toying with Emily, Daniel was back to kill her as well.

She was alone, on a deserted highway, in the dead of night, with an insane murderer who had just tried to run her over and crush her.

This is absolutely insane, she thought.

She came to this realization in almost an instant, her mind flooded with adrenaline from the energy she had just picked up moments ago while excited that she could finally be back out on the road. Now she realized she had put herself in harm's way by doing so. Once the realization had worn off, she witnessed what happened in front of her. Daniel, in his attempt to run Emily into the ground, had missed and had instead bounced off the metal barrier, and the car lurched back onto the highway, at which point Daniel hit the brakes hard and brought the car to a stop.

Emily watched as something shook in the car, and suddenly, the wheels began to smoke against the asphalt as they moved rapidly backward. Daniel was backing the car toward her, she realized.

He was coming back in for the kill.

In a moment of panic, she decided to sprint forward.

Emily realized that trying to move away from the sedan would actually give the driver more room to make a better hit against his target. If, however, she closed the gap, perhaps Daniel wouldn't be able to turn quickly enough to successfully make the collision. He would either have to turn so sharply that he would back straight into the metal barrier, stopping him completely and possibly damaging his rear axle, or more likely, he would try to keep his turn shallow and miss her completely.

It worked. She closed the gap, and the sedan backed up right past her, bouncing off the metal barrier again.

Emily didn't give up on this amazing opportunity. She ran as fast as her exhausted legs would allow. Every muscle and joint in her body already ached. But she wasn't going to give up now. Not now.

Not ever.

As she ran forward, she could hear behind her the sedan switching gears. It was revving up, and he was going to try to run into her again. But as luck would have it, she'd run so far down the highway by this point that she managed to reach a part of the forest where the trees started to thin out a little. Suddenly, she found a place that she could actually jump into without having to navigate thick trunks or brambles.

The car was directly behind her, gearing up for another run at her, ready to run her over.

Emily wasn't about to look a gift horse in the mouth. She used the opportunity.

Feeling the heat of the high beams almost directly upon her, Emily stumbled toward a downed tree, and with a swift leap over it, she was back onto the soil and clambering deeper into the trees.

She had barely gotten into the forest when she heard the car speeding away, accompanied by the sound of Daniel screaming into the cold night air.

To Emily, it sounded like somebody on a roller coaster ride or winning some kind of competition.

The bastard was enjoying himself, she realized. This was all just a game to him. He was having fun.

He was actually having fun torturing her as she was trying to make it back home.

Holding back the tears of her situation, she grabbed onto some of the surrounding trunks and pulled herself deeper into the forest. She was going to continue south, but she was going to go through every thick, dark patch of forest that she could get away with.

She didn't care how long it would take her to walk through all this. She wanted to be hidden. She needed to be safe.

As Emily walked, she pulled her phone out for short bursts, using her flashlight on and off to illuminate her way through the forest.

Briefly, she considered the possibility that whenever she made these quick illuminations in the forest, Daniel would be able to see them and would be able to know how to find her. However, Emily dismissed this idea as a ridiculous notion. Daniel had driven away and was not constantly following along the side of the forest. Even at a snail's pace, if he had been doing that, Emily would've been able to hear the engine starting and stopping over and over again.

Ever since she dove into the forest, Daniel probably didn't know exactly where she was. It was extremely likely that he had a general idea of where she was, based on how fast she could walk through a thick forest and his own experience of following her thus far. But she knew that if she stayed in here long enough, her chances of losing Daniel would slowly increase. Perhaps there was some good sense in not tempting fate, but realistically, Emily knew that flashing short bursts of light in the forest wasn't going to alert Daniel.

Emily was more concerned that a light going on and off in the forest might actually alert any wolves or coyotes in the area. She really didn't have enough experience with the animals to know how they reacted to light in the night. She wasn't sure whether, when she came upon a coyote, flashing a light in its eyes would frighten the creature away or irritate it and make it angry. These thoughts were why after an extended period of walking through the forest, Emily decided that using her flashlight wasn't a good idea.

That, and the fact that when she last looked at her battery, simply by walking around and using the flashlight, she had drained an additional ten percent of her battery power. If she kept it up, her phone wouldn't last very long at all.

So the phone went back into her pocket, and she was alone in the darkness once more.

Maybe it was the fact that there was a killer in a car trying to come after her. Or maybe it was the simple fact that Emily was now surrounded by dark trees in every direction, even high above her head. Even the stars couldn't have illuminated anything through the canopy of leaves and branches. In any case, Emily found herself more isolated than ever before. It was always lonely walking down the highway, but at least that way, she could see the world around her. Stuck in the forest, she felt like she was grasping and toiling through an unending void of darkness.

Emily knew that if she kept this up, if she didn't do anything to change her current situation, she might put herself into such a deep claustrophobic panic that she might even go into shock. She needed something to hold onto. She needed some kind of mental stability.

It was at that moment, when she reached back into her pocket to pull out her phone, she realized there was something else in there.

Her earbuds.

Her earbuds with their own built-in AM/FM receiver.

She barely even remembered that they had that feature. Her phone had a satellite radio feature and could pick up not only any station her earbuds could, but several more from all around the world. In fact, she couldn't recall ever even once using her radio receiver.

Now, however, lost in the depths of the forest, about to go stir-crazy from being locked away in the darkness and her phone becoming useless due to its lack of connectivity, she realized the earbuds might, in fact, be her only hope.

Ignoring the fact that she had only moments earlier been struggling to preserve electricity, and desperate just to hear another voice that didn't berate her femininity, she plugged in her earbuds and flipped on the switches that connected her to the radio waves. And despite everything working against her—like being able to pick up radio waves in the depths of a dark, enclosed forest—it actually worked. She actually got a little bit of an FM signal.

She immediately set it to the same radio station she had listened to in the car earlier.

". . . which obviously wasn't expected, but the family was grateful that they could all be brought together anyway. Mark Stevens for local news. Tracy?"

"Thank you, Mark. This is Tracy Galloway for local news, and if you are just joining us tonight, we are continuing our report about the status of local infrastructure repairs after a mysterious signal outage, which as many of you are understanding right now, I'm sure, has effectively plunged the entire region into a blackout area in which no electronic signals from any Bluetooth or wireless devices have been functioning for quite some time. As we have mentioned earlier, there is currently no further information from local law enforcement as to the nature of the blackout, why it was caused, how far-reaching it could be, or any other such data. However, we did receive confirmed reports from the mayor's office *that he is authorizing the release of several city workers to work around the clock in order to set up emergency transmitters to allow the city and surrounding regions to regain their online capabilities and get all of our people back to work as soon as possible."*

Emily's heart sank. It was exactly what she was expecting, but she still didn't really want to hear it.

The reason her phone wasn't working wasn't because of a bad data plan or some stupid feature from her old phone. There was something wrong with the cell grid system. And by the sound of it, the entire grid system over the entire region. It wasn't that Emily couldn't get a phone signal. It was that nobody could get a cell phone signal. Of all the rotten luck, Emily realized, on top of everything else happening to her—like the breakup, the harassment, and somebody nearly trying to run her over and kill her—the reason she couldn't do anything about it was because on this night, of all nights, the grid system chose to fail.

It was all she needed at this point.

Although she reminisced out loud, there was one, ever so slight, bright side to hearing this kind of news. Now that she knew that there was no hope of using anybody's cell phone to get back in touch with the world, she wouldn't try to ask anybody if she could use their phone. Wouldn't be much of a point if they were all not working. All she needed to do now was find a way to get back home. The only priority.

The only way she was going to stay alive tonight.

Tracy Galloway continued on the radio. *"Obviously, that is the major headline that has been dominating people's minds over the course of the night, since it's going to be affecting quite a lot of people tomorrow. We've heard reports of many landline services having trouble making more than simple local connections. In fact, reaching out to every possible website has become difficult even in our own radio offices. So we encourage everybody to take a step back, take a deep breath, and realize that people are working around the clock to be able to bring the services back and realize that this may be a wonderful opportunity to get back in touch with human connectivity, whether that be with your family, your friends, or your neighbors. Just being able to speak with them face-to-face, maybe invite them over for a chat, play board games, these are things that have been lost with our online generation."*

"Thank you, Tracy. Now we return to another story that we have been following. Tracy, what have you uncovered regarding the grisly discovery of the bodies found in West Edmonton?"

"Thank you, Mark. As we reported earlier this evening, the body of Cynthia Richards was identified almost immediately, due in part to her having ID on her person when her body was found. We have just learned from police that thanks to some investigative work, they were able to identify the second body as that of Sally Eldridge, who was only recently reported as missing after—"

Emily turned off the earbuds and put her phone back into her pocket. But not before checking the battery power.

It was barely half-full at this point.

"Stupid, stupid!" she whispered to herself. Obviously, if the flashlight was going to be a drain on her power, then the radio certainly would be as well. She really wasn't sure what she had been hoping to accomplish by listening to the radio. Sure, it had provided her with some human voices, but nothing she could interact with. Really, all the news report could do was let her know that the power outage was region-wide, not just isolated. She should've turned off the radio immediately after that, she knew. Hearing more about the murders wasn't really going to provide her with anything other than more paranoia.

She was just so desperate, under the circumstances.

And she figured it was causing her to do some pretty ridiculous things. Like putting earbuds into her ears while being chased down by a maniac along the highway. The last thing she should be doing at this point, she realized, was blocking out her hearing with even the smallest amount of distraction. She needed to be able to hear; she needed to be able to know what was happening. After all, it wasn't like she would hear any news about herself or Jeremy. That had only recently happened, and if the media had even picked up on a local roadside death, then the police certainly would have, and there would be a lot more cop cars all along the highway.

Nothing Emily did while wandering through the forest made any sense. It was like a badly written chapter in her life. And she knew it was all orchestrated by some damn simpleton who'd specifically gone out of his way to torture her.

And now, thanks to the use of her phone battery, she was potentially in a worse state than ever before.

12

E mily continued struggling through the blackness of the dark forest, heading south along roughly the same line that the highway traveled.

Right up until she couldn't.

Up ahead, the trees started to thin out and provided her with a little bit of a view, opening up into the night sky. At first, Emily didn't understand why the trees were starting to split apart until she came in for a closer look.

She had reached the tree line, where the trees could no longer grow or extend forward. The ground dropped off suddenly into a shallow cliff. What few trees attempted to grow into the edge of the cliffside had clearly had their roots exposed thanks to the ground's natural erosion. There were a few trees that started to miraculously grow sideways out of the cliffside, plus the odd shrub. But overall, the cliff was far too sandy and far too steep to support anything as heavy as a tree.

Looking down, Emily could see that the drop was easily a good five or so stories into the valley, which housed a decent-sized river. To her left, Emily could make out, in the starlit night, a concrete bridge where the highway was located, which she needed to follow in order to get back home. It was the bridge she needed to use to cross over this river and continue her walk back to Edmonton.

And even a cursory glance told Emily that it was the only bridge within sight. It was the only way to get across without going for a swim.

Emily tried to remember crossing this bridge on her way north earlier. At the time, she was obviously thinking about other things, like how her boyfriend could do something so horrible to her as to cheat on her. She had been rather destroyed at that moment. Road directions certainly weren't on her mind, particularly since it was virtually a straight road going all the way up toward Legal. Vaguely, she did remember crossing over a river, though the valley didn't seem quite as deep that first time around. Maybe it was because she wasn't paying attention. Maybe it was because she was in a car and drove by it quickly enough to not care about the details.

Maybe it was because she had never seen it the way she was seeing it now, directly in front of her, staring straight down into it.

"Easily five stories high," she said.

She looked around at the side of the cliff but couldn't see any kind of trail or easy way to go down. Plus, the cliff was largely made of sandstone, by the looks of it, very soft stuff, very beach-like. If she attempted to go down that way, she would almost certainly slip down and go falling into the valley at top speed. She would never survive. Add to that the problem of how she would have to cross the river—probably freezing cold—and then find a way to climb up on the other side, and the entire ordeal didn't seem worth it.

No, if she ever hoped to make it back home alive, she would have to do so via the highway bridge. Realistically speaking, she would have to do so pretty quickly. She knew if somebody was trying to run her down, she wouldn't have a lot of options in getting away from them while crossing over the bridge. But given what she knew was out there, she figured she would find the energy to make a quick sprint across the bridge, maybe even allow herself to rest on the other side if she could find a safe place.

Walking along the forest line up against the cliffside, she kept moving, at the best place possible, back toward the highway. She figured this was the best way to go since it gave her a little bit of extra light this way, where the forest had cleared. Plus, she could actually keep an eye on the road and see if any sedans were patrolling it.

Eventually, she reached the point where the forest started to move back north again, transforming the sandstone underneath her feet into a collection of gravel, probably the remnants of the construction that had originally been used to build the bridge in the first place. It would only be a detour of maybe ten feet, at most, before she actually had to hop over the barrier and be on the highway again. Moving her way back toward the barrier, she realized she was actually going upward at a slow pace. Apparently, she remembered even less about this bridge from her northern excursion than she had thought. Immediately north of the bridge, the road sloped slightly upward, climbing to a higher elevation and making a slight hill.

Emily stood there, realizing that if she had walked the entire distance on the highway asphalt, she would've had a reasonably relaxing downhill slope to walk on. Maybe there was a downward slope the way she went, through the forest darkness, but it wouldn't have been noticeable, given all the rocks and leaves and brambles she had to step over and the unevenness of the ground in general. Overall, she didn't feel like she had gone downhill, and psychologically, it felt like just as much drudgery as the rest of the evening.

Just one more thing to add to my long list of complaints, Emily thought.

She almost felt like she wanted to kneel down and cry. Everything, literally everything, was going horribly wrong for her this evening. But she knew she couldn't stop. She knew she still had a long way to go.

Desperately trying to think back to coming this way earlier in the evening, she wondered how far from Edmonton this bridge was. She knew she was past the halfway point, but how far past the halfway point? Did she still have a third of the way to go? Maybe even just a quarter? She didn't know. It was hard to remember. But however much distance she needed to cross, she knew she still had a long way to go with some asshole trying to run her down somewhere along the way as well. There was no time to waste.

Turning toward the bridge, she started her run.

Now completely out of the trees, she could feel the beads of sweat running down her body as she ran, pulling up a little bit of dirt and soil she had collected and mixing them with the dried blood, infesting all of her scratches and cuts. It really began to sting. Also, the pain of the stings only compounded the exhaustion she felt in her legs, trying her best to run at a fast pace across the bridge when she had already walked dozens of miles, or what certainly felt like it, driving her leg muscles to their limits. She hated every moment of this, but she didn't really have a lot of options. This was the worst night of her life.

She had gotten about halfway across the bridge when she could feel sharp pains going through her stomach and up her leg. She had completely cramped up the left side of her body. Slowing down to limp, she used the opportunity to brace herself against the bridge side rail and look out over the river.

It was a beautiful star-filled sky, illuminating the shining waterway underneath her, surrounded on all sides by sandstone cliffs topped with enchanting forests. It was a beautiful sight, and in any other circumstance, Emily would be grateful to be here to see something so wonderful. She even hoped she would want to come back here sometime in the future and enjoy it without having to worry about anything else.

But the thought occurred to her that, given what she was going through right now, maybe she would be so traumatized by the experience she would permanently associate it with Daniel. She didn't want to think about something like that. She didn't want to live that way. She didn't want to give this asshole the satisfaction of making him a part of her life.

Still limping and trying to pick up the pace, she got almost across the entire length of the bridge when she looked down over the barrier on the other side. From this vantage point, she could see that the cliff on the northern side of the bridge was, just as she had seen at the forest line, very steep. For whatever geographical reason, however, the cliff on the other side, the south side of the bridge, was much less so. Over there, it was almost at a forty-five-degree angle. Certainly nothing to shake a stick at. If she had slipped while walking down something like that, she would've slid down the entire way. But at least it was a comparatively manageable climb. It wouldn't have been an instant death if she had fallen off something like that. Luckily for her, she never had to find out the hard way, since she hadn't actually climbed down the north side of the valley.

Staring back over the bridge and looking out across the valley to the north side, the side she just left, Emily realized that there was something there. Something on the bridge.

A car.

A sedan.

But it wasn't working; it wasn't powered on. It was coasting.

There was a downward slope on the north side of the bridge portion of the highway, and this car was using that downward slope to quietly coast toward the bridge.

Directly toward her.

13

W hen Emily finally realized what was going on, at that perfect moment, the horn suddenly started blowing extremely loudly.

Emily panicked. She completely freaked out. She had no idea if this was going to be Daniel, leaping out of the car to shoot her. Or maybe start the car and run her down. Or maybe some other situation she wasn't expecting. She didn't care. Enough was enough. She didn't want to deal with any of this anymore.

Terrified of what was coming and startled by the sound of the horn, Emily leapt over the barrier and plummeted off the bridge.

Fortunately, by this point, she had crossed nearly the entirety of it and only fell about ten feet or so when she hit the sandstone underneath.

The soil gave out underneath her. She slipped and tumbled down the side of the hill, down toward the river.

Everything was black; everything was spinning. Emily wasn't sure which part of her was still facing the ground and which part of her was aiming toward the sky.

At some point in the tumbling and the loss of control, Emily suddenly felt a sharp bludgeoning to her rib cage and realized she had slid down into a sapling strong enough to stop her in her tracks. Her body flipped around the south side of it and continued to slide, but slowly.

Now, at her slower pace, she reached out desperately and grabbed onto some brambles, cutting the palms of her hands with the spiky thorns. She managed to pull herself to a complete stop.

She only got to breathe for about a second before she heard it, coming from the bridge above.

"Are you okay, baby?" cried Daniel in a sarcastic, mocking tone. "Did you fall? Do you have an owie?"

There really wasn't any time to lose. Maybe Daniel didn't see where she landed or where she fell, but maybe he did. She immediately pulled herself directly into the brambles, slicing up her clothes and her skin even more than before, held her breath, and kept as still as possible, completely covered in shrubs.

Somewhere up above her, there was nothing but silence and then the sound of a door slamming. Some footsteps, and then the sound of his voice coming from up the hill. "Hey, you didn't fucking die this time, did ya?"

She heard him trying to walk down the sandstone and then slip and curse. She heard him scramble back up, still saying, "Shit," and, "Fuck," before trying to climb his way back down the hill again, and then cursing again as he slipped some more. Finally, in his frustration, Emily heard no further walking.

But out of the corner of her eye, she saw a very powerful light scan the hillside. If he wasn't going to find her in person, he was going to try to find her using a flashlight in the dark of night.

On one occasion, the light clearly showed exactly where she was. She wondered how much of her could be seen in the thick shrubbery she'd pulled on top of herself and desperately held her breath on the off chance that her breathing might somehow give her away.

Finally, after what seemed like forever, the flashlight moved away, and she could see it shaking up the hill as Daniel tried to climb back toward the bridge. He was climbing away.

All the while, she could hear him say, "Fucking bitch, she probably fell in the fucking river. What the fuck?" And with that, he rounded the concrete barrier and made his way back to his car.

Emily lay motionless underneath the sharp brambles until she heard the engine of the car come back on and heard the car drive away.

Then, and only then, did she crawl out from underneath the shrubbery, grimacing in pain at every cut her flesh endured, and began to slowly claw her way up the soft sand, back toward the road.

The climb back up the hill took up the better part of a half hour. It was certainly a lot easier going down than getting back up, but Emily was still amazed at how difficult the climb actually was. The sandstone kept giving way underneath her and sliding her down several feet for every step she had gained. She tried to reach out in the darkness and find any bit of nature that she could hold onto that might help her pull herself back up. The brambles weren't really that much help, since they were filled with thorns and nettles, and they constantly cut into her palms, stinging them and filling them with splinters. The sapling that she had originally hit with her rib cage and that had slowed her down was a bit of a help. It was surprisingly sturdy in the sand, and she was able to use it to pull herself up a good distance, even getting her footing on it and pushing herself up farther. She hoped it would be able to support her weight without breaking underneath her. Emily didn't want to think that she had destroyed a nursery ecosystem in her attempts to get away from Daniel.

She just didn't want to give that bastard the satisfaction of anything anymore. She didn't want him to be responsible for making her do such awful things.

Eventually, she managed to climb her way partly up the hill until she reached a part of the soil that started to get comparatively thicker than the sandstone, possibly clay or even sedimentary rock. Feeling around with her fingers, she found a stone imbedded in the soil and desperately clung to it, struggling to use it as a way to leverage herself out of the ground. It was hard going, considering that she couldn't actually see where she was grabbing in the dark. She couldn't make out the shapes of the stones or whether there were even more helpful stones to begin with.

The thought occurred to her that she could probably pull out her phone and use her flashlight to be able to see where she could go next. But almost immediately, she nixed that idea. Firstly, there was the problem that she had to grip the cliff with both hands. She worried about slipping all the way back down to the river if she let go of one hand for too long. Secondly, her hands were now covered in so much blood, sand, and clay that she was worried if she tried to reach into her pocket and pulled out her phone, she would lose her grip on that as well, and then she'd lose her phone in the dark, maybe even directly into the river. Then she would really be out of luck.

And then, obviously, the third problem. Daniel was still out there. He was driving around, looking for her. At this moment, he theorized that maybe she had drowned, that she was dead. On the off chance that he was close enough to see the area, she didn't want to give her position away by turning on the flashlight.

No, she had to do this, and she had to do this in the hardest way possible. She gripped her fingers back into the soil and continued to climb.

Eventually, she got to a point where she was able to hoist her body up onto a high enough stone by bending in a way she certainly wasn't expecting to ever be able to bend. She pulled her feet up to where her hand was and pushed herself upward. Then, balancing precariously on the cliffside, she reached up, felt around, and grabbed onto a sapling at the top of the hill. She pulled herself up with what little strength she had left, hoisting her body back onto grassy, level soil. She was pretty confident that she had snapped the sapling in the process and had probably killed the tree. At this point, she couldn't have cared less. She wanted out. She wanted out of this mess.

Finally pulling herself onto the flat land, she lay on her back and stared up at the starry night sky and allowed herself a moment of respite, breathing in deeply now that she was out of the valley that she otherwise didn't know how to get out of.

Sadly, off in the distance, she could hear a car engine. Daniel.

Fear fueling her blood, she jumped to her feet and made a mad dive for the forest at the side of the river, jumping immediately into the trees and hiding in the darkness of the branches.

Daring to look out of the trees to make sure that she wasn't spotted, she wanted to know if he was going to be crazy enough to drive his car into the forest or maybe pull right up to the edge of it and simply come out and kill her with his bare hands.

To her surprise, the car actually drove on.

Then she got a quick look at it and realized it was a pickup truck. It wasn't the same car. It wasn't Daniel.

By all accounts, it could've been somebody who was good enough to pull over and give her a lift back into the city. Only now, it wasn't going to happen. She had missed her chance.

She was so desperately terrified of the prospect of running into Daniel again that she had completely ignored the possibility that someone else might've pulled over to help her. She never even considered it.

A chill came over her body. The idea of being safe had long ago left her mind. And now, the result of that was that the first car that had come by, the first car that might have been able to help her, had driven on by, and she had missed her chance to get any help from it.

Emily swayed and fell back into the darkness of the forest. She leaned down against a large tree trunk and slid all the way back down to the ground, sitting uncomfortably on a bunch of roots as all the courage and spirit she possessed left her body.

And then, for what must've been the tenth time that evening, she began to cry again. Only this time, she just couldn't find a way to make it stop. The tears flowed from her eyes, and she had neither the strength nor the motivation to stop crying.

There wasn't any point to any of this anymore, was there? Emily couldn't see a reason she should tell herself that everything was going to be okay. She couldn't find any reason to believe that if she stopped crying this time, then she would be able to move forward and find a much better solution to her current predicament.

Why was this happening to her? she thought. Then, just to make sure it was real enough, she spoke up and asked herself, "Why is this happening to me?" She really couldn't understand it. She hadn't done anything to anybody. Nothing with any serious results, in any case. She couldn't remember ever harming anybody or being horrible to anybody. For most of her life, she was always an awkward and geeky kid, always doing a lot to make other people like her, and generally being very passive and submissive. The perfect kind of person who would be accepted by most. Certainly not the kind of woman who would garner any ire from anybody.

Frankly, the more she thought about it, this was the reason she'd ended up having a pretty steady boyfriend beyond college in the first place. Jeremy. Jeremy, this hot, kind of interesting guy who, if they were still in high school, would never have given her a second look. They had both been adults when they started dating in college, doing more adult things like drinking and having sex. They talked; they discussed schoolwork and pop culture and other supposedly 'adult' and 'sophisticated' matters. It seemed like it was a nice ride.

In this sense, Emily felt that her characteristically supportive nature was actually beneficial to the relationship. She was always very agreeable, always wanted to do everything Jeremy wanted to try. Whether it was at a club, or seeing some new place, or in the bedroom, she was always open and willing to doing whatever it was he wanted to do. She just wanted to have a nice, stable, happy relationship. She wanted to be a good girlfriend.

And everything always felt as if it was going wonderfully. There was never a complaint.

Which, Emily realized in retrospect at that moment, was probably part of the problem.

People in relationships didn't just accept what the one partner wanted. People in relationships usually had differences of opinion and worked out their troubles and communicated to see if there was a solution that they could arrive at that would help out the both of them. By any stretch of the imagination, if Jeremy had a problem with the relationship, he probably would've spoken up about it. At the very least, he would've broken up with her.

Emily now realized she had allowed herself to believe that those were all indications that the relationship was going well, that there wasn't a problem, and that their relationship had entered a certain degree of repetitiveness and standardization, as many long-term relationships do, or people just get comfortable with each other. She told herself that the quieter and more boring things were, the more serious they really were.

She'd never once stopped to consider that maybe, just maybe, the reason Jeremy wasn't saying anything was because he was hiding the truth from her. Maybe he was enjoying his little girlfriend on the side while having his current "girlfriend" pay half of his rent. Or maybe he simply got off on the idea that he was a successful cheater. Some sort of machismo, celebrating his manliness of being so deceptive and filled with guile. A real charmer, a real playboy.

Or maybe in this case, the simplest solution was probably the correct one. Maybe, if Emily was being honest with herself, Jeremy was just a coward. Maybe the reason he got himself a little college girlfriend was because he never grew out of those sexy college days. And the reason he didn't break up with his old girlfriend was because he wasn't the man he thought himself to be and just didn't have the strength and the courage to do it.

And Emily had just let him walk all over her.

She wondered what she'd done to deserve that kind of treatment from Jeremy. She wondered if it was some sort of character flaw or some sort of decision that she'd made about her life. Maybe, if she could identify it, she would realize what it was that she'd done to make a guy like Daniel think that he could get away with doing whatever he wanted to do.

And then, just as quickly, Emily snapped herself out of it.

There really was no justification for Daniel's actions, she told herself. She didn't even know the man. She didn't know anything about him, where he'd been, what he did, who he really was. He was some random asshole who had been turned down in a bar. It wasn't like he was the first human being ever turned down in a bar before. Did he really think that all the other guys out in the world went and tried to run down the women who'd turned them down as well? Surely, they couldn't all take rejection this badly.

Surely, all men weren't animals like he was.

At a certain point, there had to be a moment when a man decided that, okay, he'd tried his best, and he should just move on. Learn from his mistakes and be a better man for it. Certainly, not go out of his way to inflict harm on another human being. Certainly, not think that he got to play with a toy.

The reason Daniel was acting this way, if Emily had to determine a reason, was simply that there was something desperately wrong with him. He was a deranged lunatic, a psychopath. He thought his stupid act at the bar would make women swoon, and when he was given a reality check, he didn't know how to react to it.

And unfortunately, he currently had the power to act out his little fantasies.

There was nothing Emily could do to stop it under the current circumstances. She understood that. But maybe the situation was similar in the case of Jeremy, Emily started thinking. Maybe he, in his own way, had been under the impression that he was entitled to do anything he wanted. And maybe she'd enabled him, gave him the power to feel like he could screw around and play around all he wanted.

Maybe she'd left him feeling as if he was completely right.

And therefore, the reason his relationship with Emily was failing was because it was all Emily's fault.

Emily finally stopped crying.

Maybe she should stop feeling like a poor little victim. And maybe she should finally stick up for herself against these sick bastards.

14

Emily got up and continued walking.

With the experience on the bridge long behind her, she decided that there was no time to waste and no reason to live in fear anymore. She decided she was going to face it head-on. It might result in an attack, but frankly, she'd been attacked all night, and she was tired of simply rolling over and letting it happen to her. This was the night she was going to make a stand. This was the night she was going to get home safely and get to the police.

Maybe there would be a serious danger with her going to the police. But the more she thought about it in her exhausted state, the more she arrived at the conclusion that it was probably not going to be the case. Things would probably work out in her favor if she were to go to the police.

One, a proper forensics team would be able to determine that the deaths of Jeremy and Erica had been caused by circumstances that were outside her control. They had suffered through a car crash, and they had received injuries using weapons. Definitely knives, possibly a gun. None of which she had on her person. None of which she ever had on her person, and if the crime scene was investigated, they would soon discover that no such knife or gun ever existed with her prints and couldn't have been thrown away anywhere. Also, if she would actually approach the police in the first place and make the report initially, it would look far more favorable to her than if the police found the bodies without her. After all, there would be no good reason for her to turn herself in.

Emily was aware that this was kind of a long shot. After all, her DNA was at the crime scene from when she stuck her hand into the car. And certainly, DNA of Jeremy and Erica was on her from when she got covered in the blood. But she had to believe, deep down inside, that since she didn't actually do anything wrong, the police investigation would reveal that as well. If they did their job properly and if they looked through the evidence, they would determine that the DNA of the killer was probably on Jeremy and Erica as well.

Point number two. There was the extremely real fact that she was being harassed and hunted by a crazed maniac all over the road. The next time she got out onto the road, she would make a point of trying to remember the license plate number, a detail that she regretted she had missed every single other time. Regardless of what the police thought about her, if her explanation, if her alibi, was that she was being chased by a crazy loon, they would be obligated to at least look into it. They would look for his car, and they might determine that he had been hunting her. They might even match the car to the one that struck Jeremy's car. Perhaps they might even look inside his car and quickly find his weapons. Again, a bit of a long shot, but she did have to trust that, again, the woman who did nothing wrong would be determined to have done nothing wrong, and the guy who went out of his way to purposely do everything wrong would surely be found guilty.

Emily had to believe that. And she had to believe that the system she lived with her whole life actually worked.

And yes, she was guilty of engaging in a fight in a bar. That much was true. But even in that, perhaps somebody would be able to identify that it was where she'd met Daniel for the first time and that he had been following her ever since. Again, a bit of a long shot, but it really was all she had to go on at this point. Even if she got arrested for starting a fight in a bar, it would've been worth it just to get somebody involved who would be able to put a finger on Daniel.

Assuming anybody saw anything . . . or if they were even willing to help her . . .

No matter. This was already a nightmare situation. All Emily wanted was to get to a place of safety right now. And if that meant getting into a holding cell, then so be it. At this point, it would've been far preferable to have gotten picked up by somebody, anybody, for any reason, even if it was an arrest, than to have to deal with everything that had been happening to her this entire night.

She knew she was losing quite a lot of time by taking extra precautions, however sensible they might have been. In order to get back to Edmonton safely, she would really have to get a move on. And that would mean leaving the safety of the forest. Despite the fact that the trees were thick enough to stop any car and also dark enough to keep her hidden in the night, it wasn't the straightest or quickest way back to Edmonton.

Ultimately, she decided the best approach was to compromise and have the best of both worlds.

For what must've been a few miles by now, Emily had been walking backward. Not entirely, but with enough reverse action to allow her to keep a good eye on the road.

Effectively, Emily had decided to walk in the same manner that a lot of hitchhikers do, constantly changing from a forward-facing position, quickly switching around to walking in reverse in order to stick out their thumb toward any car that was passing by. The latter part of which, of course, was irrelevant. She didn't need to be a hitchhiker at this point. She wasn't expecting any cars to drive into town this late at night. She wasn't expecting to get picked up anymore. More so, the priority was to be able to keep a forward-facing position while still having a good view of the world behind her.

Emily realized that in most of the encounters with Daniel, it was always from his car coming up behind her as it was travelling south, in the same direction she was walking. It made the most logical sense. It was the side of the road that was closest to her as she was walking with traffic. The point being, she was continually walking on the right side of the road, and if Daniel ever wanted to get closer to her, he would have to drive up on that side of the road as well. In the few instances when he'd ever had an encounter with her on the opposite side of the road—in which she was walking south, but he was traveling north—the most he could ever do was yell to her from a distance.

Emily reached an area of the highway where the forests were constantly in close proximity to the side of the highway. Also, there weren't any ditches here anymore. The forest areas were effectively encroaching on the highway, only stopping a foot or two from the metal barrier. Emily realized that the forest would make for a pretty quick getaway if she needed one. Hence, the reason she was walking down the highway on the wrong side of the metal barrier. If she ever did catch a glimpse of Daniel, she would be able to quickly run into the forest.

She was obviously running the risk of being caught by Daniel, but this was still a reasonable middle ground. The forest was close, and she had a good chance of being able to jump into it before being spotted. And even if she were spotted, what could Daniel really do? He certainly couldn't drive into the trees. And would he really chase her into the forest to get her? Her experience at the bridge showed her that he was a slightly portly, clumsy man. He wouldn't be able to run after her through a forest. He didn't seem comfortable coming out of his own safe zone. She was willing to bet he wouldn't want to leave his car.

By all accounts, it made for a pretty good getaway plan. Or as best she could muster under the circumstances.

After a little while of walking this way, she caught a glimpse of a car driving up over the horizon, completely black, with no lights on, attempting to coast as quietly as it could.

She was certain it was him. And he was very deliberately trying to drive as quietly as he could. As was his modus operandi by this point.

She jumped into the trees.

She was diving headlong into the darkness of the forest when she suddenly remembered—she still didn't have his license plate number.

She was planning on getting access to his license plate number so that she could report him to the police. Given her vantage point, that would make it pretty difficult. She'd have to go deep into the forest darkness in order to be safely hidden from Daniel's view. Perhaps she could go closer to the edge of the forest, to the tree line, but then she would run the risk of being spotted. Considering how this man had been talking about her this entire evening, it was a risk she was not willing to take.

Then she came up with a brilliant idea. She would climb a tree.

Halfway up a pretty decent birch, she began to realize what an incredibly stupid idea this was. She was now trapping herself up a tree that only had one exit, back down to the ground. If Daniel spotted her, he would be able to trap her there. And frankly, he was a larger person than she was. Even if he was portly and clumsy, there was a very realistic possibility that he would be able to climb the tree after her.

But reaching a very high branch, she realized she was in the thick of it. The car was about to drive by, and there was no turning back now. On top of that, it was only once she reached the high branch that she realized that this wasn't necessarily the highest tree in the forest. It certainly wasn't high enough for any climber to be able to look out over the forest canopy. If anything, it was much harder for her to see what was going on from here than on ground level.

Of all the bad decisions she'd made this evening, Emily determined that this was by far one of the most boneheaded.

And then, on top of everything else, her spine went cold when she heard Daniel slow his car down and bring it to a full stop.

What was he doing?

She watched as he stepped out of his car, walked into the forest . . . and then pulled out his phone.

And then she watched as he was using his phone.

He was tapping away at the screen. He was moving it about like a GPS locator.

He actually had GPS.

Which, on a cell phone, Emily knew shouldn't be possible since there wasn't any cell service. Even the radio news report from earlier had reported that nobody had any cell service in the area.

So how the hell did he?

She watched as he tapped away on the screen and kept getting closer and closer and closer.

Until he was finally standing underneath the very tree that she had climbed, effectively trapping her.

He turned his head skyward and looked directly at her.

Then he laughed.

15

"I see you," Daniel said, quietly taunting her. And then, his small laugh turned into a much larger one as he continued to giggle and snicker and stare at her the entire time, practically drooling on himself.

Still laughing, he turned on his heel and casually went back to his car. He climbed in, started his engine, and drove away.

He had me, Emily thought. He had her right where he wanted her. He could've done anything. He could've shot her from the ground.

But he came out here, very deliberately, just to let her know that he could find her.

He was toying with her. He probably could've killed her several times over this evening. But this was all just a game to him.

Emily sat up in the tree for quite a while.

She knew it was completely idiotic that she was in a tree. It wasn't any safer of a vantage point than anywhere else in the forest, and it entrapped her. If Daniel had decided to climb the damn thing, he probably would've gotten her into a much riskier situation. He could've easily killed her, and there would've been no way for her to escape except maybe sliding down from the thing and risking breaking a leg on God knew what was on the forest floor at the moment.

But more than that, she knew it was absolutely idiotic that she didn't get down from the tree either. Daniel already knew where she was. He could come back anytime he wanted, and she would still be there.

Daniel was able to find her with ease.

She slowly climbed down the tree. She wondered if whatever bad luck she'd been experiencing would keep things going by having Daniel show up at that precise moment she touched the ground.

Fortunately for her, nothing of the sort happened. Taking a breath and looking around to get her bearings, she began her trek through the trees once more.

Now that Daniel had proven himself to be capable of tracking her reasonably well, giving him the opportunity to do so by walking on the roadside where she'd be spotted would be a foolhardy idea. Instead, she decided to stick to the darkness of the forest. Sure, it was much slower going, but at least this way, she wouldn't be easily seen.

While trudging through the forest, Emily started thinking about how he was able to look for her so casually and actually find her in that tree. She hadn't made any noise, and she hadn't rattled any tree branches, causing leaves to fall on him. So how had he done it?

She recalled how Daniel had moved slowly and methodically toward her tree, tapping on his phone. That was the key. He'd tracked her on his phone.

Which meant he had some form of tracker installed on his phone. Probably some kind of GPS signal.

Somehow, even with the cell phone outages and the internet outages, Daniel still had a working phone.

There was something about that that did not add up.

She tried to recall when her phone had stopped working. It had been working on the way to Legal. She had used it to track down the signal on Jeremy's phone to figure out where he was. So everything had obviously been working prior to her going into that bar.

So the first time she could actually remember her phone no longer working was when she'd tried to call for help with her car. That was when the internet and cell service went out.

She had contemplated going back into the bar to use a landline, but she was scared they wouldn't let her. She had been worried the bartender would call the cops on her for the confrontation and throwing things.

As her mind replayed that incident, she recalled Daniel hitting on her as he came from the door. But when she'd come in, he'd been seated at a table. She recalled thinking then that he was kind of creepy. Still, she hadn't paid much attention to what he'd been doing while she was having it out with Jeremy.

Wasn't it a little coincidental that her car and her phone stopped working just as she met him? That everything happened just as Daniel entered her world? In the time she was in the bar, had Daniel zipped out, damaged her car so that it wouldn't work anymore, and maybe . . . shut down all the cell towers?

It sounded crazy. Maybe even just a little desperate. And under any other circumstance, she would tell herself that it really didn't make sense and that it was a stretch of the imagination. But then again, she also had the evidence of the rest of that evening. She also had to consider the fact that Daniel had spent several hours after that chasing her in his car. So was he the kind of person who, seeing her walk into a bar and get in a fight with her boyfriend, would quietly excuse himself just to damage her engine and also shut down any means of her being able to reach out to anybody? The same guy who haunted her by driving around and calling her names and sneaking up on her in a tree just to laugh at her? Then the answer was yes.

Daniel was absolutely the kind of loon who could do something quite this insane.

Emily wondered what kind of person had the ability to shut down cell service and internet for an entire region.

There must surely be people who could use services without the need of cell towers or internet services. The army came to mind. Or maybe someone with a walkie-talkie or CB radio would be able to communicate long distance. And landlines too. There were those still available, not that she knew of anyone who still had one other than businesses.

The question was how was Daniel perfectly prepared to be able to use his phone even without those services?

To Emily, it all seemed just a little too coincidental. Just a little too suspicious.

The timing of it all. The fact that he was using his phone to find her. The fact that this guy had a deranged quality about him. Everything was pointing to the idea that some-how, Daniel had arranged all of this.

He had been waiting for her in that bar. Well, maybe not her specifically, but someone like her. He was waiting for some woman to come in just so that he could shut down the phone services and disable her car in order to entrap her. To take advantage of her.

To threaten to kill her.

Emily was fully aware that Daniel could probably pick her off at any moment, and he was biding his time, playing with her, torturing her, terrorizing her for his own reasons. And he wanted her to know that he could do it.

He could run her down; he could shoot her; he could violate her and strangle her in the middle of the forest. He could do anything he wanted. He knew how to find her. But how? Could he have bugged her phone?

Emily frowned. That wouldn't have been possible. It had been on her. Did he somehow figure out how to ping her phone, like she did with Jeremy's? How could she stop him from doing that? Turn it off? She pulled it out and shut the phone down completely. It wasn't much use anyway, and she didn't want to ditch it. She needed her phone, but she would do what she could to shut down his chance of getting to her. Hopefully.

All right, you psycho, let's see you find me now, Emily thought. *And if you do somehow manage to track me down again, I'm going to be ready.*

16

It was still dark despite the illumination of all the stars. However, when Emily turned and looked behind her, she felt very confident that she was able to see out on the horizon the curve of the hill that led toward that bridge she'd crossed some time ago. She thought she could still see the area of the forest where she'd climbed the tree to get away from Daniel.

She, of course, was probably wrong. There weren't any lights to give her any indication of what was actually around her. On this darkened part of the highway, everything looked pretty much exactly the same as everything else. There really was no telling how far she had traveled.

She didn't think it was very far, even though she'd been walking for what seemed like hours since leaving that tree. The problem was that her legs were sore, and her feet were practically numb, and she was barely limping along now. It took great effort to just lift her feet from the ground to move forward. Not to mention the tumble she'd taken down the cliff and the blood she'd lost.

The thought of blood turned her stomach as she recalled

Jeremy's and Erica's bodies covered in blood. She shook her head, trying to clear her thoughts from that unpleasant scene as she focused on the road again, which was off to her side.

The forest had ended, and she was now in a large stretch of grassland, probably somebody's farmland. Emily hadn't been certain that she was moving anywhere at all except for the fact that the trees behind her were growing farther distant. Her head was sort of foggy, and she was feeling the exhaustion of the past several hours. She had never walked so far in her life. She wondered how long she'd actually been walking. Was it getting close to sunrise? The sun would be nice. It would allow her to see farther ahead. Of course, that also meant she'd be visible to Daniel, who was still out there somewhere, hunting her like a crazed psychopath.

Emily had abandoned the concept that once the sun came up, she would probably be safer from Daniel. If anything, at this point, the sunrise was more like a ticking time bomb. All of Daniel's control over her largely hinged on the fact that he was able to do whatever he wanted, whenever he wanted. The sunrise would change all that.

She fully expected the highway to be more frequently used by drivers. The fact that she hadn't seen any drivers for quite some time told her that no matter how busy this highway could get, at this hour practically the entire region was sleeping. The odds that there would be a late-night trucker still driving at this hour were getting slimmer, and those odds weren't working out in her favor this evening since she hadn't seen anybody for quite some time.

But once the sun started to rise, then the early bird employees would be heading off to work. Meaning that, all in all, this place would start becoming far busier than it had been all night. She didn't care what time it was or how little internet access the region had. Business wasn't going to stop over something like this, and even if it was the slowest day of the week, somebody would be on the road by the time the sun rose.

So there would be more traffic getting in Daniel's way. And there would be more opportunities for witnesses because it would no longer be so dark. Somebody would surely see him.

And she knew it. And what was worse, she knew that he knew it.

He was sadistic and cruel, but he wasn't an idiot. He had spent the entire evening hunting her down and harassing her, and she knew what he looked like and where she'd seen him the previous night. It wouldn't be hard for her to identify him to the police. And she knew he knew that too. Therefore, his only option was to finish her off and never allow himself to be identified or caught.

Emily knew that Daniel was working on a deadline, that he was toying with her and torturing her. But eventually, he would have to start getting real and finish her off.

But that just brought her thoughts back to the fact that she didn't know what time it was or how long she'd been walking. She had no idea how much time she had before the sunrise. She had no idea how much time she had before Daniel would start getting desperate to kill her.

She knew he would be, though.

She suddenly realized that she hadn't actually seen Daniel since he'd found her in the tree. It was probably the longest stretch of time she'd had without him interrupting her.

But why? she wondered. Did he actually get scared and run off? No, he'd gone too long and too far to give up now. The thought that maybe he had lost her crossed her mind. Maybe he couldn't find her since she'd depowered her phone. Of course, she wasn't sure if her phone was still giving off a signal that he could track or if he was somehow able to do it by detecting heat signatures. Or any other number of possibilities she couldn't even begin to imagine.

No, she decided, the most obvious answer was probably the correct one in this case. No matter how well Daniel planned everything out and no matter how much of an advantage he had, he still had to give way to the laws of physics. His car probably needed gas after driving up and down the freeway all night long.

It was a brief respite, she decided, but it wasn't going to last her very much time. Barely a reprieve.

And then all that time of being away from Daniel, Emily was confident that she'd barely made any distance in her walk. *What a waste of an opportunity*, she thought. She really must be getting delirious from blood loss if she honestly thought any of this was a good idea.

Case in point, in her current condition, she decided she needed a weapon. Preferably one that didn't rely on batteries.

Part of the matter that delayed her rather extensive walk was the fact that she was constantly looking down at her feet, trying to determine if there was a stone among the gravel just off the highway that would be large enough, and sharp enough, to use as a hammer or a knife. Anything that could give her even the slightest bit of an advantage. But no dice, she realized. All the rocks along the road were too small and too soft. They might as well be sand.

Looking down constantly, she realized that at a certain point, the rocks started to become clearer and easier to see. She didn't really have any explanation for this until she looked up and saw that, wandering down the highway, staring down at her feet, she hadn't noticed the incredibly obvious.

She had arrived at a rest stop, one with a lot of lights.

With what little energy she had left, Emily practically galloped toward the building and looked around the area.

She couldn't see a payphone or anything that resembled a landline. There weren't any people stationed at these kind of rest stops. It was just a building with bathrooms and vending machines, a place for travelers and truckers to stop and take a break in their driving.

It would have to do.

Leaping over the metal barrier separating the rest stop from the surrounding brush edge of the farmland, she decided to look for a weapon, maybe something a trucker or passerby dropped or threw out. She got on her knees and rooted around in the brush. After only a little bit of time, she found something that might be somewhat useful to her.

A long, straight stick. It looked as though it had come from one of the large tree branches that overhung the area. It was decaying a bit with age but still pretty sturdy, Emily determined. Also, given its reasonably straight shape and lack of any knots or smaller branches sticking out of it, it kind of reminded her of a spear. Except, of course, that there were no sharp edges on it. Both ends of the branch looked pretty dull.

It will have to work, Emily thought.

Grateful for even the smallest opportunity to stop walking, she came back out to the rest stop area and looked around the gravel. She didn't have to search very long before she found a piece of rock that was sharp enough to be used as a primitive blade. Not a very good one, it would never be able to slice open flesh. But with enough force, Emily decided that it was good enough to be able to go at the end of the branch to turn it into more of a spear. She began sharpening it simply and primitively, like somebody would with a pencil if they had a knife and nothing else.

She sat down on the edge of the walkway to the bathrooms. It wasn't the most comfortable, but it felt good to get off her feet. She worked on making the end of the thick stick a point. She was glad that she'd found something that she could use against Daniel if he showed up again.

The thought had barely crossed her mind when the familiar sedan pulled into the rest stop and drove toward Emily. Wherever it was that he had gone, she could see that he was back to harass her or worse.

She wondered if she was ready. She was exhausted, delirious, dehydrated. And she suddenly felt that a sharpened stick wasn't really going to make a lick of difference. Especially against a guy who had already proven he wasn't afraid to run her over.

That said, she was certainly going to act brave, even if she didn't feel it was very sincere.

He pulled right up to her and put his passenger-side window down again. He leaned over and looked right out at her. "You doing okay?" he asked. "You're not looking too good."

She just stood there, grasping onto her spear like it mattered. She had no idea how to deal with this situation. She wasn't looking so good? How did he expect her to look after everything he'd done?

"So you're not gonna answer?" he finally added. "Come on, why don't you just get in the car? I can give you a ride home."

Son of a bitch was treating this like it was normal. She gripped onto her spear, twisting it in her fingers, ready to stab him if he attempted to get to her. After everything he had done, he still had the nerve to be casual about everything.

"Come on, you stupid bitch," he said, rolling his eyes. "There's no fucking point anymore. Just get in the fucking car!"

Emily didn't say anything, just gripped her spear tightly. She didn't wanna hear any of that, but at least it sounded more familiar.

"Look," Daniel added, "I'm the one who slipped the photo under your door. I know where you live, okay? I can give you a ride back."

Emily almost dropped her spear. She didn't want to move. She didn't want to give anything away. She didn't want this bastard to know that her entire body had gone cold and she was about to fall over, go unconscious, go limp, start crying.

He knows, she realized. He actually knew where she lived. He was the one who slid the note underneath her door. The note that warned her that Jeremy was cheating on her. The note that started all of this.

Meaning that he had been following her for ages. That he'd involved himself in her life for, easily, weeks or even months. That this was all a sick and twisted game to him, and he had been playing it for a very, very long time.

How in the world? she thought. How was she going to deal with something like this? With this insane lunatic who had been harassing her and planning this evening around her for months?

All of a sudden, standing there with a sharp stick really started to feel like nothing at all. She was in way over her head, she realized.

And unfortunately, in the time that she had spent thinking about this, realizing how out of her depth she really was, Daniel evidently got frustrated at listening to her silence.

"Yeah," he said with a sigh. "Enough of this." And with that, he reached down into his car . . .

And Emily could hear him cock the hammer of a gun.

17

Emily knew it, dammit. She had been absolutely certain that she was right, and she was.

The asshole had a revolver. And he was the one who splattered Jeremy's and Erica's blood all over the windshield of Jeremy's car.

Emily had brought a stick to a gunfight. She was woefully unprepared for this.

With a massive leap, she threw herself to the side of the building and ran, then tripped and tumbled down into the brush of the farmland. Somewhere behind her and over her head, a few bullets rang out through the night. Daniel had tried to shoot her. He'd really tried to end it all for her right then and there.

"I love you," he taunted in the night. "You know that this is all that love is ever going to be for you! Guys are like this! Sooner you realize it, the better! This is just what love is!" Then he drove off into the night once more.

Emily looked down. In the tumble toward the farmland, she had rolled over her stick and snapped it into two pieces.

There was nothing she could do to change this. She felt

more helpless than this broken stick. She realized that all her careful planning and exhaustion had amounted to nothing.

She continued walking. In all the time she had walked, the sun still wasn't anywhere closer to actually rising.

Emily began to wonder if she was so exhausted and so delirious from the blood loss, dehydration, and all the walking she had been doing—not to mention nearly being killed several times over—that she had completely lost track of time and distance.

Was she even sure anymore that she had been walking for hours? Her body certainly felt like it had been. But how could it take this long for the sun to rise? But maybe it had only been a few hours, not nearly ten.

In her present state, how could she be sure it hadn't been merely minutes? How far did she actually get down this highway? Had she imagined that road sign to Morinville?

Did she really get anywhere at all?

Well, if any of that was true, she thought, then she had completely lost her mind. She had lost any semblance of distance and time, and for all she knew, she was walking in circles or in a completely incorrect direction. Maybe Daniel was really just some demon sent to torture her soul while she walked through this hell. Or if she was still alive, maybe he was the Grim Reaper. And he was slowly coming in closer and closer until, finally, he would be able to capture his quarry and take her up to the next life.

These were the thoughts that raced through her head as she became increasingly woozy. She was sure she would collapse at any moment.

Frankly, she determined that she probably would've collapsed several yards back if not for the broken stick that she continually leaned on.

The stick, which had been pretty long prior to her breaking it, was now short enough to reach up to just under her shoulder. And it was still pretty sturdy, all things considered.

She was now in a state where she was delirious and felt completely helpless. She could be run over, or he could shoot her at any moment, and she could barely stand up without the help of a broken stick. And she couldn't even trust her own memories at this point.

She began to review the events that had happened to her with a little more scrutiny again, if for no other reason than to wonder how quickly she could jump out of the way the next time he decided to fire a gun at her.

And the more she thought about it, the more Emily realized that something didn't quite add up. In their last encounter, he'd fired the gun at her.

Daniel had a gun. And he'd had her in full view.

And he hadn't finished her off.

Something about that didn't make sense. There was really no way, Emily figured, that she should still be alive.

So what was it? What was the piece that she was missing?

She thought about it. Daniel had a gun, and he was comfortable with using it. Adding the fact that he had been comfortable when he drove past Jeremy's car, like he knew what had happened to them, indicated to her that even though it was circumstantial, he was the man who had shot Jeremy, killing him.

Now, did he shoot Jeremy while driving his car? Emily thought. It was an important point, after all. Because if he did, then it meant he was able to fire into a moving vehicle from another moving vehicle and hit the driver. Not an easy task. Even if he had shoved the car into the ditch before he shot Jeremy, there would've been a struggle unless he shot them before he assaulted them and then sliced them up. Probably the most reasonable explanation. If he had a gun to use against two people, both of whom could've overpowered him, then why wouldn't he? Why wouldn't he play it safe?

Which meant that Daniel had to be an accurate shot with that revolver. And he could've easily shot Emily. Yet he didn't.

Emily also considered that Daniel could've stepped out of his car and gunned her down. After all, why not? When she'd leapt off the bridge and fell down the cliff, he pulled over to look for her. When she'd climbed the tree, he pulled over to track her down.

So why not this time? Why didn't he just get out of the car and finish the job?

She wondered about that for a moment. He could have killed her in the forest, when she was up in the tree, but he didn't. He walked away. And he could have gotten out of the car and come after her a few minutes ago and murdered her, but he didn't. Daniel had had the opportunity to kill her and then simply chose not to do it. And in the matter of his getting out of his car to walk around to find her when she'd leapt off the bridge, well, he hadn't really put that much effort into it either. Why didn't he fire off a few warning shots to scare her? Why did he simply want to confirm that she was still alive?

And then she thought, how did he miss running her over?

She was an exhausted woman. He was a psychotic behind the wheel of a car. Could he really miss at that distance? Could he really miss backing up into her?

She had always taken it for granted that Daniel was purposefully toying with her, to simply torture her, make her feel terrified that she was being hunted down by some lunatic. But looking at it more carefully, she realized that this was taking torture to a whole new level. He wasn't being nonchalant about messing with Emily. This was his entire purpose. It was his modus operandi.

Which, the more she thought about it, the more it made

sense in her mind. Here, she was dealing with a guy who had been following her, stalking her for what was probably weeks or even months. He could've easily kidnapped and raped her any time he had seen her before. He obviously didn't. He'd obviously put a lot of effort into toying with her and psychologically destroying her.

Maybe, she considered the possibility, maybe killing her wasn't his goal. The only problem with that was that she couldn't reason how he was going to get away with any of this if he left her alive. More than likely, killing her was probably just the unfortunate end result of playtime. His real goal, his real intention, was to enjoy making her afraid. It wasn't something he was just doing before killing her. It was what he definitively wanted to do. He had planned it; he had anticipated it from day one.

Torturing her was his ultimate goal. It was the goal he had been working toward, the only thing he had dreamed about.

He knew this was going to happen from a long time ago. This was his plan. It was practically his life's mission.

What if he was so confident in what he was doing this evening that he felt he could get away with anything?

Literally like a cat toying with a live mouse, batting it around before eating it. What if the only reason Daniel deliberately missed his perfect shots, deliberately walked away from finding her in the tree, deliberately acted as if everything was going perfectly well between them this evening . . . was because he knew that no matter what he did, it would always work out for him?

What if he had complete and absolute overconfidence, without even the slightest bit of doubt in his mind?

What if this was his playground, his orgasmic little fantasy? What if he was a kid playing with a toy that would never harm him or turn against him?

She considered the analogy. What if a little kid was

playing with a toy with complete confidence, one that could never harm them . . . but then they accidentally bumped themselves in the head? What if they actually did get hurt?

In that situation, Emily reasoned, it would be such a shocking wake-up call to the child that he would be startled with pain and wouldn't know what to do with himself.

What if she had given Daniel too much credit because of his GPS? What if he was just a sad little boy playing?

And what if he were taught a lesson in reality?

Up ahead, Emily spotted a portion of the highway that had a slight turn. There was a metal barrier to prevent any cars from speeding off the road at the turn and flying off into the forest up ahead. The barrier looked stronger on the curve than the rest of the barrier, like it was reinforced more.

Perfect, she thought.

She took the stick she had been using to hold her up and snapped it over her knee, dividing it up into reasonable arm-length sticks.

She crossed over the barrier to the highway side and dug out a hole in the dirt, deep enough to shove the dull end of the sharpened stick into the soil. Covering it over with more gravel, she now had a diagonal spike sticking out of the ground.

Then she got up and dusted her hands off. She stepped out into the highway, standing out in the road, directly in the sight line of any driver who would come after her.

And she waited.

She didn't have to wait long. After only a few minutes, she heard Daniel rev his engine behind her, trying to terrorize her some more.

She didn't turn to face him, didn't acknowledge that he was there. She didn't want to make him think that there was something odd about her staring at him as he drove right into her. She was hoping that he wouldn't, that he wasn't finished 'playing' with her. She was counting on it.

She wanted him to think that maybe she couldn't hear him. That maybe he was getting lucky and had caught her by surprise. She wanted Daniel to think that she had no idea there was a car behind her, driving right at her, until the last possible moment when he would turn away from her.

She wanted him to come at her full speed, none the wiser.

Hearing the engine roar behind her, she knew he was only about ten feet away when she sprang into action.

Emily knew that Daniel didn't want to kill her. He wanted to get as close as possible to her before veering off right back onto the road. But she also figured that he would want to get as close to her as possible before turning away.

Which meant that if he was this close to her, and if she gave him just enough time to see her diving toward the right, toward the ditch again, then he would compensate by turning toward her just a little. Not enough to run her over, but just enough to head in her direction before turning away.

Just close enough to drive directly into where she was standing.

Directly in front of the spike.

There was no room for error with this one. But at this point, she wasn't willing to put up with any of this nonsense anymore.

Even death would've felt like a victory at this point, Emily thought.

At the perfect moment, she jumped out of the way, and just as expected, he drove a little in her direction to compensate.

And he drove directly into the spike.

His front right tire burst, and he continued to drive forward at a high speed, with a flat tire, losing control of his car.

Emily fell to the ground hard. But she propped herself up quickly enough to watch as Daniel's car veered off, drove onto the gravel shoulder, and collided with a concrete post on the curve of the metal barrier.

After going so fast, it was horrifying to watch it almost stop dead as its rear wheels lifted off the ground before coming back down hard. Glass shattered from the windshield and continued flying forward as Emily watched airbags explode inside the car and flood the front area of the sedan.

She didn't check to see if Daniel was injured or unconscious. She didn't run up to him to kill him off and finish the job. She never even considered the possibility of looking for his working phone.

Instead, in a moment of panic, Emily did something that she would later regret, that was probably the stupidest decision she'd made this entire evening.

She ran.

18

Emily attempted to run as best she could. The insides of her shoes began feeling as if she were walking on some sort of gelatinous surface, like bubbles. It also felt like she had sweated through her socks.

In fact, Emily had been entirely confident that she had simply bled through her socks after the blisters on her feet had begun to burst. She hadn't dared to remove her socks or her shoes during the entire evening of walking. She didn't want to risk the possibility of getting her wounds covered in gravel and any other particles found along the highway and getting herself infected. She didn't want to have to suffer anymore.

God only knew what her feet looked like after she had stepped in that bog water earlier that evening.

But all things considered, she could clearly feel what was going on in her shoes. And more certainly than anything else, she could feel the pain. Every step was like dipping her feet into acid. Except only particular points on her feet. On one foot it was the heel. On the other, the ball of her foot and the toes. As the night wore on, she walked so much, she was certain that the blisters had begun to spread to other parts of her feet, the parts of her feet that she was desperate to walk on when everything that she had walked on up till that point had become so painful, so disastrous.

And now she was running. Yet she could barely feel the pain.

Somewhere behind her, the ground was slowly becoming less illuminated. She assumed that the remnants of light she was seeing must've been from the front lights of Daniel's car. Which was a bit of a surprise, seeing as how, currently, the front of his car was pointed in various directions, having just crashed into a concrete slab at the edge of the highway.

She was amazed that the lights were working at all. It seemed to her that the front of the car was probably totaled.

Running still, she turned her head quickly and saw the scene she was leaving behind. Indeed, the front of his car had crashed into one of the concrete slabs that were holding up the black highway guardrail. It wasn't a full-on frontal collision because the front right tire of the car had burst, causing the car to swerve awkwardly before colliding with the concrete. She could still see how the car was leaning over, no longer having another wheel on the right side to keep it even.

Hard to imagine it staying even in its current condition, anyway. A portion of the front of the car was now completely caved in, mangled metal barely concealing the destroyed right side, revealing the engine innards. The opposite side of the car had surprisingly fared better, with its lights still working and bouncing off the reflectors on the metal barrier. That must be the light that Emily saw tracking her feet as she was slowly running away from the car.

Within the car's interior, all she could see were the large white outlines of the airbags. With the front windshield of the car smashed into splinters from the crash, the front window was left wide open, expanding the airbags outward. It enveloped the entire view.

Emily couldn't see the driver.

It was, unfortunately, also the furthest thing from her mind. All that mattered now was that she knew where the light was coming from. The car's left front light. She also knew it wasn't moving or expanding. It wasn't closing in. In fact, it would never close in again.

For the first time in this entire situation, Emily found herself completely assured that the car would not be coming after her.

It was over. *It's actually over*, she thought.

Running fast and hard on her painful feet, she felt the cool night air blowing in through her nose as she raced southward down the highway. It was the first time she had run so far and so fast and so hard for many hours. The gentle aroma of the surrounding natural world and the farmlands was clean.

It smelled clean and beautiful.

She felt like every horrible thing that had happened to her this night was being scrubbed off her body in the night air.

It was over. It was actually over. Daniel couldn't get her now.

As she ran harder and faster, she could feel the cramps starting to come back into her body. Walking so long and so hard earlier, she had developed cramps in the side of her waist, in her calves, her arms, and her neck. She had developed pain that had become so familiar, it was amazing to her that she had almost forgotten that her body was feeling pain at all. She had grown accustomed to it. It had become her new normal, living with this pain.

But now the euphoria of the experience was starting to wash away, the adrenaline starting to fade, the endorphins washing away with the smell, and the pain started to return to her body with a vengeance. She remembered why she was lumbering and walking so slowly down the highway for so long by now. The pain was in every joint of her body, destroying what muscle tissue she had left, burning every ounce of fat on her bones like gasoline.

Suddenly, she was reminded of what it meant for her body to hurt as she walked down the highway. And it hurt like hell, from her head down to her blistered toes.

She looked back down toward her feet and could no longer see the light emanating from Daniel's car. As she was starting to stumble in her run, she managed to bounce back onto her feet as she stuck her arms out in a desperate attempt to balance her position, keeping herself from falling.

Regaining her balance, she dared to look behind her one more time, just to prove that it was real.

The light was still shining from the front left of the car. It was still active. But it was very distant now, fading into the night. The outline of the sedan could still be seen, mangled and destroyed against its concrete slab. But it was starting to blend into the night as well, slowly becoming less visible the farther away Emily ran from it. After another few yards, she figured the only part of it she would still see would be the faint white of the airbags, which still didn't look like they had moved during the entire time she had seen them.

She turned her gaze forward again and found another burst of energy with which to sprint. She was confident that the car was no longer going anywhere, and it fueled her muscles and joints. She wondered, ever so briefly, whether that smell of gasoline was actually pouring out the front of the car or possibly what her body smelled like when she was burning so much energy. As if it were real combustible fuel.

It has to be over, she thought. It must surely be over.

As she headed farther down the highway, rounding a

corner, Emily realized that the ground sloped downward, and she began to stumble again. Now, having run so long and so hard, she no longer had the energy to try to straighten her balance, and she allowed her body to fall down onto the gravel beneath her feet, tumbling to the hard ground. Amazingly, she could still feel the ground sloping downward—she didn't recall ever actually running up a hill. Though, in the tumult of the entire evening, she had to confess that she really didn't remember what she had been running on all this time. She allowed gravity to take her as she rolled down the slope.

She felt like surrendering to it, like letting the gravity of the world take her heavy weight and control it. She could finally let everything happen to her, out of her control.

Because she believed she was safe to do so.

After this long, hard evening, of everything happening without her permission, without her consent, suddenly, everything was finally over. She could feel in her mind that everything was over. If she surrendered her body weight to the world around her now, if she let her body fall, if she let the dirt get into her wounds, if she let the pain overwhelm her, if she let the tears pour forth from her eyes again . . . for the first time in a very long time, she felt she wasn't going to be harmed, she wasn't gonna be killed.

She was free. She was free to be herself again.

She felt her body roll down the shoulder of the highway until it reached the natural end and just rolled to a stop. Letting her arm stretch out, she lay on her back and looked up at the sky.

Somehow, she imagined that maybe there were fewer stars in the sky. Maybe it was because night would soon end, and all in due time, the sun would finally start to rise.

She couldn't believe it. It was actually, finally, over.

She felt the weight drifting away from her body, sinking

into the ground beneath her. She could feel the coolness of the rocks underneath her skin, smell the breeze of the rural air blowing across her. Her eyes adjusted to a few beautiful stars that were still hanging in the night sky.

And she started laughing. And the laughter grew into a howl.

She didn't care if any wild animal heard her now. She didn't care if a legitimate car suddenly showed up out of nowhere and passed her by. All the dangers of the world could overtake her now, for all she cared. She laughed so hard, filled with mirth and pleasure. Everything inside her screamed with joy.

She was free, she believed. She was actually free from Daniel.

He was dead.

. . . He was . . .

Emily shut up, and her body calmed again. She realized to her shock that in the panic she'd felt from having successfully crashed that car, she hadn't actually stopped to check to make sure he was dead. Also, she'd never actually seen him during any time she looked back at the car while running. His airbag was too large and covered him.

By all accounts, maybe he was still alive.

Maybe he would wake up and start all over again.

And if, somehow, she managed to get to the police before he woke up—hell, even if she got to the police and he still somehow died—how would it look if she explained to them that she had fled the scene of an automobile accident?

Another crime to add to her rap sheet from this evening. Being a public nuisance. Assault. And now, fleeing not one, but two auto accidents. One of which she'd stuck her hand into, covering herself in her ex-boyfriend's blood.

The other, if she were being completely honest, she'd caused.

Emily slowly dropped her head into the palm of her hand. She was worried, but then the slightly more rational part of her brain kicked in. She was a victim of Daniel's, she'd been scared for her life, knowing he was going to kill her, that he more than likely had killed Jeremy and his lover, and the police weren't going to arrest her for trying to get away from him.

Despite that rational thought, she knew this nightmare was far from over. She still had to make it home so she could call the police. And she still didn't know whether Daniel was alive or dead. So her nightmare of a night wasn't over yet.

Not by a long shot.

19

Emily sat in the darkness, wondering what she should do now. Should she continue her journey home? Should she go back and check to see if Daniel was actually dead?

There was a very real possibility that he was dead, that he was either dead or dying behind the wheel of his car. Maybe he had crashed hard enough against the steering wheel that it cracked his skull and he'd not be waking up ever again. She seriously hoped that was the case.

Or maybe he simply had a concussion and had passed out. That thought actually scared her because it meant that he could still come after her, still track her.

She had detected the smell of gasoline pouring from Daniel's car. Maybe it would catch fire with him in it. Any spark would set it off. Maybe she wouldn't have to worry about him coming after her. Not if he was set ablaze.

Emily didn't like the idea that she was turning into the kind of person who would be pleased by the thought of Daniel roasting to death in his car.

In all likelihood, Emily had to concede that his airbag

had worked and that he was simply injured and unconscious, but very much still alive, behind the wheel of his car.
And when he finally woke up and realized what Emily had
done and how much she had cost him to his car, and
possibly his health, he would be after her with a vengeance.
Or worse yet, if he woke up, realized what she'd done and
that he had been proven inferior by a woman . . . she didn't
even want to imagine what he'd do to her if he caught her.
Truly, the worst insult that a man of his pathetic caliber
would ever wish to live through was to be proven inferior to a
woman.

He would wake up completely enraged. Vengeful. Bitter.
Murderous. And still carrying a gun.

It seemed to her like going home was the last place she
should even consider going. Particularly since she had no
way of calling the police there since she didn't have a
landline.

But then again, Emily thought, *Daniel has a working phone.*

If she did go back to the car, she would have to deal with
the possibility of Daniel's state, whether he was alive or dead.

Which meant that by doing so, it would be the second car
with a dead body in it that she'd stuck her hand into. That
wouldn't exactly look very good on a police report, but these
were extenuating circumstances.

And of course, this was all assuming that Daniel was
either dead or dying, like she secretly hoped. There was
always a possibility that she would go back to the car, either
wait for a police car to drive by or risk sticking her hand into
the car to find his phone. And in either circumstance, she
could discover that he was, in fact, alive. Maybe he had
crawled out of the car and planned to surprise her from
behind as she waited for a passerby. Maybe he would realize
somebody was trying to get his phone, and he would grab her
instantly and have her in his grasp.

And it would be a dangerous situation that she had willingly walked into.

Emily didn't want to do it. This night had been nothing but a nightmare. The only reason she was even out here was because she'd gone to confront her boyfriend about his infidelity. *No*, she told herself. *To hell with that.* This wasn't her fault. She now knew, thanks to Daniel, that he had been stalking her for weeks. If he had never slipped that photo under her door, she would've never driven out here . . .

And she would be trapped in a loveless relationship. In a dead-end life that meant nothing.

And the psycho would still be after her.

She briefly wondered whether Jeremy would have even cared that this creep was after her.

On the other hand, Emily looked down the road and could just barely make out the green outline of a road sign. Green, indicating directions toward cities and towns, probably also indicators of how far away she was.

She wanted to know how far away she was from Edmonton. She really wanted to believe that all of this was for something.

But what if, after everything she'd been through, after everything she had to put up with from Jeremy, Daniel, and the bartender, she just lay back and waited for the world to pass her by?

Hadn't she earned that right? Didn't she deserve to have something, anything, go right in her miserable little life?

After all, what did she have to look forward to going back to Edmonton? Writing up data entry for various clients who wouldn't know what happened to her tonight and wouldn't really care as long as they got what they wanted? A waitressing job that would probably lambaste her for coming into work covered in cuts and bruises?

An empty bed?

No, she thought. There really wasn't anything there either. Just another version of living out her life, day in, day out, living paycheck to paycheck and wondering what it was all worth when she finally retired on an irrelevant pension and waited for death.

She briefly wondered what would happen if she just lay here and let the wild animals find her. Let the vultures pick her bones. Let the cars run over her, completely unaware.

What relevance do I really have in this world? she asked herself. What was it that she hoped to accomplish? She drove out all this way to confront her boyfriend in a bar, and look where that got her. She no longer had a boyfriend, and at least as far as Jeremy went, she never would. And if she had never confronted him, she would probably have lost him eventually, anyway. After he got bored with her and tossed her aside like garbage.

She turned her head back to where she had left the car crash and wondered what was going on in the mind of a man like Daniel. He obviously hated women and didn't contribute any value to her personally. She was easily dismissible, he could kill her with a flick of his wrist, yet she was still a sick form of entertainment for him. The only value she had to a guy like that was to basically do whatever it was that he believed he wanted of her.

It was how Jeremy treated me too, she thought.

Emily really couldn't believe it. She racked her brain and concluded that she couldn't think of a single male in her life who would've attributed any value to her. Not even one single guy.

She started to wonder why she was so desperate to have a boyfriend in the first place.

Oh, yes, she thought. If she sat there and delved into her memory long enough, she could block out all thoughts of everything that had happened to her this evening and just barely remember it.

Having a stable relationship out of college was just what a good girl did. It was normal. It was a standard way of living life.

And more so than anything, Emily wanted to be normal.

It was so sad, she realized. Everything that she had done, everything that she had struggled to accomplish, was all just to be a *normal* person.

She hated it. She wanted to be free of it.

But then she thought about all the instances she'd had this evening when she suddenly felt powerful and free and liberated from the horrible circumstances she'd found herself in. And the more she thought about it, the more she realized that every step of the way, Daniel was always ahead of her.

Her dreams of being a strong and independent woman, a real survivor, amounted to very little. Sure, it gave her the adrenaline she needed to live. But now that it was all wearing away, fat lot of good it did her.

She still had to go back to her regular life.

Emily sighed. She knew she couldn't do it. She couldn't just abandon the life that she had always known.

She knew it was her obligation as a moral citizen to try to report the accident. She couldn't live with the idea of walking away from that and having to explain herself to somebody when they finally found out.

She was tired of fighting.

With her mind made up, she stood up, brushed herself off, and started heading back toward the car. She needed to find that phone, and she needed to call the police immediately. She needed to explain to them everything that had happened and how it was all either in self-defense or a collection of circumstances that had gone wildly out of control. At the very least, she knew if she rehearsed it enough, she might actually start believing it.

She climbed over the small hilltop, looking back down toward the wreckage...

And saw a dark figure coming toward her from the car.

A portly man, all in black tactical gear, which looked rather childish and ridiculous on a man of his frame. And he didn't even cover his face, so it was clear who it was.

Daniel had crawled out of the car and changed into tactical gear.

In one hand, he was holding a bag.

In his other hand, he was holding his revolver. Ready to fire.

And he was walking away from the crash. And in her direction.

The moment she gasped in shock, he looked up and saw her.

Emily had decided to do what society told her was morally right and simply follow the rules. And it had become, once again, the stupidest decision she could've made.

She had just closed the gap between herself and her stalker.

He seemed astounded that she was there, right there, ready for the taking, when suddenly, he stopped shivering and stared at her in violent rage, baring his teeth. "I'm gonna kill you, bitch. Get over here! I'm gonna kill you!"

He pointed his gun toward her. She briefly caught sight of his hand swinging, probably from the crash, before she turned on her heel and ran as hard as she could.

She heard him fire the gun and somehow found the energy to run harder.

Running toward the road sign was now out of the question. It was a wide-open space on the highway. It would make it easier for him to shoot her.

She darted to the right and dove immediately into the forest, running through every branch and bramble. Somewhere along the way, she lost her shoe and could feel her blistered foot get flooded with infectious waste.

Another gunshot rang out, and the bullet hit a tree somewhere behind her. She no longer cared about her foot.

She ran as hard as she could, deeper into the forest.

Somewhere behind her, she could hear Daniel screaming, "Where the fuck do you think you're going? You're not getting away from me this time! You can't escape me!"

20

Emily wasn't sure what the best course of action was. All she knew for sure was that she didn't have a lot of time on her hands to debate the issue.

She figured that if she made the wrong choice between two options, she would end up having her stalker and potential killer come upon her. But even if she made the right choice, she figured it wouldn't be long before he ended up closing the gap between them anyway. All she really knew for certain was that if she didn't decide something soon and stood still, it would be a death sentence.

She didn't want to dismiss the severity of what had been happening to her by thinking of it as just something that happened, but she did have to acknowledge to herself that up to this point, she knew what to expect. She had a good understanding of what Daniel wanted, what Daniel was going to do. She was expecting him to show up on the road in his car. Obviously, it was terrifying, but it wasn't surprising.

But the situation she was in now? This was new. And this was haunting.

She had to wonder if she should continue running or stop

and stay quiet. Both options had their benefits and potential harms. And both were constantly ready to fail her.

The obvious choice was to run. Emily knew this. She was in the depths of a dark forest, and there was a crazy, psychotic murderer trying to track her. If he managed to actually get his hands on her, she would be dead or possibly even worse. So she had to keep widening the distance between them. No matter where he was, she had to keep moving forward, guarding left, sneaking right. She had to keep in motion so that he would never be able to get close enough to catch her.

The obvious fact was that Emily was far superior to Daniel in running through the forest, after all the experience she'd gained this evening. Daniel probably fancied himself a big, strong man, but he had a learning curve to overcome first. She could practically hear him behind her, struggling over every rock and branch, scared to move forward so he didn't bash his nose into some tree trunk and fall over, hitting his head on a rock. He was being very slow, and from the sound of it, Emily knew he didn't like it one bit.

So at first glance, it seemed like the obvious answer for Emily was to just keep running. Just keep surviving. Unfortunately, her time spent in the forests of the rural area had certainly taught her a thing or two about being out here and being stalked by this horrible man.

For one, there was a reason animals stepped quietly when they traveled through the forest. They knew that there was a lot in the forest that could make noise. The faster Emily ran, the more she destroyed, the more she connected with. The more sound she made. With every sprint, she destroyed the leaves under her heels and moved the world around her.

She knew that Daniel was determined to catch her. She knew that he would spot even the slightest movement. So no matter how much distance she put between them, as long as she was running frantically as fast as she could, he would still know, at least vaguely, where to go to eventually catch her.

Compound that with the fact that she was on her last legs. She didn't know if she'd be able to keep running for much longer. She had to keep taking breaks, if for no other reason than just for her safety in the forest. She simply didn't have the energy to outrun Daniel to the point where all his determination wouldn't have been able to spot her. There would always be a certain degree of proximity. And Emily felt that they both knew it.

The alternative to running, of course, was to hide. If she got to a point where she felt that maybe she'd escaped Daniel's watch far enough, she figured that she could duck somewhere, possibly underneath some distant tree, stop moving, and keep as quiet as possible. Maybe, just maybe, if Daniel was determined to find her, he would be so determined that he would blow right past her, convinced that he had to chase her to close the gap. There was always a possibility that he would lose her.

But Emily figured that this would be a bit of a long shot. Sure, she'd hidden well enough from Daniel when she fell off the bridge, but at that time, he either didn't have his GPS service yet, or maybe he just forgot about it. Since then, he'd obviously found her when she was hiding in a tree. She couldn't be certain that turning off her phone would keep him from locating her because it was possible that he had some sort of heat tracker on his phone. If she hid, then he'd probably be able to find her anyway. And then he would be able to close the gap quickly.

Her lungs felt like they were about to collapse. Emily slowed to a crawl and ended up leaning on a rather large birch, trying to catch her breath.

She had stopped for a total of ten seconds at most before the tree she was leaning against had a good chunk of it blown off by a bullet that missed her head by inches. Somewhere from the darkness behind her, she heard Daniel laughing with glee.

Right, Emily reminded herself. *The last option. No stopping.*

He would catch her and find her. Emily knew stopping was never an option.

She continued running, realizing that the gap was close enough now that he could aim reasonably well at her. She prayed under her breath that there would be enough trees between them that he wouldn't be able to shoot her in the back.

She sped past another collection of birches and looked off to her right when she saw it.

A speck of light.

The first speck of light she'd seen since the rest stop. And it was out in the middle of nowhere.

Emily's first instinct was that it was the glowing eyes of a wolf, and she initially decided to run away from it, hoping that maybe, if it became interested in her, it might become interested in Daniel.

But as she ran, she looked to the right and realized that there was something off about the speck of light. It wasn't milky white, like she would expect from an animal's reflective eye. It wasn't any kind of white at all.

It was an ugly yellow. Like the kind of light that was made from burning a fire . . .

Or a lightbulb.

Emily turned and made a mad dash for the light in between the trees. She still didn't get out from beyond the tree line, but she saw it growing brighter as she drew closer.

And there it was. Long past the tree line, long past an empty field, was a house.

A farmhouse.

The first sign of civilization she had crossed in her journey to Edmonton this entire time.

She heard another gunshot and instinctively ran left, away from the light.

Emily knew that she was approaching the tree line, and when she ran out of it, she would be forced to run through a wide-open field. Easier to run, but nothing to protect or hide her anymore. She knew that the moment Daniel saw her out in the open field, all he would have to do was take a single shot and he would be able to pick her off, even from a distance in the dark.

If she was hoping to make it to that house, she realized, she had to lose him first.

Still running, practically heaving her legs through the forest, she heard the crunching of leaves in the forest behind her, which sounded closer and closer. Somewhere along her run, she heard Daniel turn with her, and he was now following her as she ran back toward the highway.

"Dammit," she cursed under her breath. She had no idea if this bastard genuinely had a method of tracking her using his phone. Maybe there really was a signal being transmitted over her phone, even with it turned off. Maybe she would be better off at this point just throwing it away. It wasn't doing her any good anyway, and it wasn't like she couldn't get her friends' numbers again. At least that way, he would think . . .

Emily almost stopped running, realizing what an opportunity she had stumbled upon.

Maybe it wasn't as complicated as some sort of high-tech gadgetry on his phone. Maybe it was good old-fashioned tracking. Maybe it was simply that she was running through a forest, against a star-filled sky, constantly stopping to avoid passing out. But all in all, maybe he was just following all the evidence she left behind of her run.

Maybe, she realized, all she had to do was leave behind some misleading evidence on purpose.

There was the possibility that Daniel knew which part of the forest she was running through because she was running on her bloody foot along all of these routes.

It was hard for her to imagine that Daniel hadn't seen the missing shoe on his way into the forest. So he certainly knew she was down one shoe.

So she figured, what if she lost the other one?

Running in a straight line back toward the highway, she eventually burst out from the trees, ripped her shoe off her foot, and chucked it as hard as she could, getting across the highway toward the forest on the opposite side. For good measure, she ripped off her jacket and tossed it as well, making sure it was clearly visible, marking the false trail she was leaving. The jacket hadn't been doing do her much good at this point anyway since it was just getting caught on shrubs and tree branches and had multiple rips in it now.

Hastily and as quietly as possible, she ran back across the highway and slipped into the forest farther down the road. Keeping her head low, she tried to sneak back in the direction of the farmhouse light.

She briefly heard him pass her by, heading toward the highway.

Emily stopped dead in her tracks, hoping that it wasn't gonna be the last time before she lost her life.

Slowly turning around, she looked behind her and watched, shocked that she had a perfect view of the point of the highway where she'd thrown her shoe and the jacket.

The embarrassing figure of Daniel, apparently limping from having to run through the forest, shuffled across the road and stopped to pick up the shoe. Then, gasping for air, he lumbered into the forest, still snickering under his breath.

Good, you heartless fuck, Emily thought. *Go that way. Get lost in the wrong forest.*

Leave me be.

Then she made her way toward the farmhouse in the opposite direction.

21

Emily had to concede that she had no idea how Daniel was tracking her. Perhaps he had some technological advantage that allowed him to find her, or perhaps it was far simpler than that. Maybe he just knew how to hunt down a hysterical woman running through the forest.

She wondered what kind of life a person had to live in order to gain that kind of experience.

In retrospect, Emily realized that it wasn't the best idea to throw her shoe and jacket in the exact opposite direction from where she was running. Eventually, he would figure out that he'd been played and that she'd just tossed her clothes away so that she could escape in a different direction. So he would just have to backtrack and move in the opposite direction. Even if that still somehow managed to elude him, he would only have to search around for a little while before he spotted the light from the farmhouse. It would be a very obvious signal to him. He had to assume that Emily, in her panicked state, would run toward the first source of salvation she could find.

Briefly, Emily wondered if she was actually making this far easier for him.

Well, nothing that could be done about it now. That house was still her best chance of survival at this point.

Running out of the forest and past the tree line, she found her feet falling upon soft, muddy soil. She had leapt into an irrigation ditch, just on the outskirts of the field.

She took another step forward out of the ditch and landed on equally soft soil. But this was the soil in which the farmer planted, so at least it was comparatively firmer. Firm enough to run on, at least.

She made her way, the fastest she could possibly run, toward the house.

She didn't care. She was out in the open. There was nothing to hide her, and if Daniel suddenly popped out, he'd be able to shoot her, even from a distance in the dark. She had to get to the house as soon as possible.

Emily wondered how she was going to approach these farmers. After all, she had lost large portions of her clothing, her shoes, and every part of her body felt like it had been slashed and cut by millions of branches. She was in a completely rabid state, and she felt like a wild woman running through some sort of primitive land. She was probably covered in sweat and tears and, more than likely, still covered in bits of dried blood. She imagined what she would have looked like if she still had that stick spear.

Suffice to say, while she was still in mid run, she knew she would have a hard time trying to explain her situation to these farmers or whoever they were. Right off the bat, they would probably want to call the police if they didn't immediately chase her off their land with a shotgun or something. And that was assuming these were rational, adult people. She was running off to some isolated farmhouse in the middle of nowhere, in the middle of the night. How did she know these were good people? How did she know that these were the kind of people who wouldn't harm a dazed, crazy, vulnerable woman running up to the property, far away from the prying eyes of the law?

How did she know she wasn't going to get killed the moment she arrived here?

What if it was just another Daniel?

She was so sick of Daniels. All the Daniels of the world could just burn in hell, for all Emily cared.

She burst out of the empty field and arrived at an old-fashioned fence line, largely made of wooden posts hammered into the ground, wrapped up in barbed wire. She followed the posts until she arrived at the gate, passing through it immediately and running toward the front of the house.

It appeared to be a pretty modern farmhouse. It looked like it could've been a house in any kind of suburban area back in the city. When running around toward the front, she even passed by a garage with an SUV parked out in front. The wall above the garage door had a basketball net.

This is starting to look promising, she thought just before all the lights in the front came on, and she stopped dead in her tracks.

The door swung open, and out came a large man. On the elderly side, but not ancient. Gray hair, wrinkled face, strong, worn fingers, probably from a lifetime of farming. He was even in a plaid shirt and overalls, exactly what she expected a stereotypical farmer to look like.

Her chest felt heavy. She felt like she was about to cry. She didn't need this. She didn't need to have to deal with more of this.

"Can I help you—oh, my God!" The man practically fell over backward at the sight of Emily and gripped the door frame to keep his balance. His eyes went wide, and his mouth dropped open.

Emily stared at him like a deer in headlights. She didn't know exactly what to expect. She figured that he would probably pull out a gun or at least threaten her to get off his property.

The last thing in the world she was expecting was kindness.

"Are you all right?" he said, coming down his porch steps straight toward her. He extended his arms, as if to grab her and give her a hug.

Emily wasn't sure what those hands meant at first, and she jumped back, raising her hands to block this man from getting any closer to her.

The guy got the hint and stopped coming toward her. "Whoa, hey," he said, raising his hands, "I ain't gonna hurt you. I just want to get you in the house so we can get you cleaned up. You look like you've been through hell." He slowly moved closer and offered one hand for her to grab while using his other to point back toward the door of his house. "Please come inside. We need to take care of you. I promise I won't hurt you."

His voice was warm, relaxing, almost paternal. He seemed to have a lifetime of knowing how to speak gently and soothingly. For the first time that evening, Emily felt like somebody's words were wrapping her in a warm blanket, and she could lie back and wash down a cool and gentle river, hearing those words of safety.

She knew it could obviously be an act. And she wasn't stupid enough to be unaware of the dangers of walking into a stranger's house in the middle of nowhere. But frankly, she knew what was out back, beyond the farmland. Anything could happen to her in that house, but she knew for certain what would happen if she didn't go inside.

And on top of that, Emily had to concede, it was nice to be able to hear a strong but gentle man's voice treating her kindly.

"Thank you," she barely managed to stammer before entering the house.

Inside, everything looked very modern. These people seemed to be doing just fine, financially. Either that, or perhaps this man with his rugged hands also had some home renovation skills under his belt. All in all, it was a homey little house for elderly people. The kind of house she grew up in.

The kind of house Emily knew she could be safe in.

A pair of soft footsteps could be heard coming down the stairs. A woman's voice told Emily that this man was probably married, living with his elderly wife. Emily hoped so, anyways.

"Ollie, what's going on?" the woman said as she appeared at the bottom of the stairs. "Is somebody out—oh, my goodness!" She clutched her chest and grabbed at the banister to keep from falling over.

Apparently, Emily looked horrible enough to practically give the older woman a heart attack.

"Mary," said the old man, evidently named Ollie, "this poor young thing was out on the driveway. I think she got into a car accident or something. We'd better get her some help. You think you can run her a shower?"

"Why, yes. Yes, of course," Mary said, struggling to catch her breath, not letting her eyes off Emily for even an instant. "Ollie, go into the side kitchen cabinet and get the first aid kit. I'm going to run this little lady up to the bathroom." She looked at Emily. "Is that all right with you, my dear?"

Emily had almost forgotten what a shower was or what one felt like. Her mouth salivated when she suddenly remembered that things like food existed, or medicine. Things like warmth, light, heat, stairs, rooms.

Things like empathy. And the kindness of old-fashioned country strangers.

"Yes," Emily replied, "I'd really like that. That'd be great . . . right about now."

On her way up the stairs, Emily couldn't decide what she wanted to explain to this couple. Right off the bat, their first instinct wasn't that she had done something horrible or that any of this was her fault. They simply saw a woman in need and assumed that she was in some horrible accident. They assumed the best of her. She wondered what she would have to say that might ruin this image of her in their minds.

But for now, she watched as this nice woman didn't seem to care about whatever bit of filth and dry blood she must be spilling on her lovely carpeting. All she did was reach into a side cabinet, pull out a spare towel and bath soap, and lead her to the bathroom.

She wondered if the water from the shower would feel anything like her tears.

22

Emily wasn't aware of how thirsty she was until some of the shower water hit her tongue. It had a strong taste to it, like iron. Heavy water, but filtered, like that from a well rather than the water she was used to.

If Emily were back in the city, it would taste as if something went wrong with the apartment building's water, and she would have to contact her super. Out here, it tasted like life.

The water flooded her mouth, and when she spat it out, she could feel herself spitting out mounds of dried saliva and blood. The next batch of water she took to her mouth, she used it to gargle and also coat the length of her throat. She knew it probably wasn't safe to drink lots of it, but she got down a third gulp of water. She'd never felt thirstier.

After that, she began getting rid of all the funk she had collected over that entire evening. The soap that Mary had provided for her was fresh and new, and she used it to wash away all the filth, the bog water, and the sweat and the tears off her face before moving to the rest of her body.

After she finished washing, she noticed a bottle of store-brand shampoo that she had never heard of, but she quickly used it to clean her hair. It was actually a painful experience, like her scalp was covered in so much dirt and grime that it had practically latched onto her and refused to leave without a fight. Nevertheless, she felt like she was washing away every painful memory of the evening.

This actually felt normal. This actually felt safe.

Around her, the bathroom seemed pretty clean. They did have some indication of dirt around some of the corners, which Emily expected from a household that was surrounded by farmland and miles away from any town. After all, these people were elderly and probably didn't get out to civilization much. They probably also didn't entertain guests. Emily figured that they kept things very simple here, very pleasant by their own standards. This was the kind of place they could get comfortable in.

While showering, Emily was fully aware that she was about to ruin it all.

Somewhere outside the door, beyond the sound of the shower water hitting her body, Emily could hear the voices of Ollie and Mary discussing the situation. She couldn't hear exactly what they were saying, but under the circumstances, it wouldn't be hard for her to figure out what the subject matter was—how to deal with her. After all, she had just wandered into their lives in the middle of the night, easily a few hours before sunrise, covered in blood and looking distraught. The way they had been talking when she was in front of them, they seemed to indicate that they believed she was in some sort of an accident. She wondered if that was really what they believed now that they thought she was out of earshot.

At the very least, Emily knew she had to tell them as much as she could and set the record straight. Somewhere, out there in the forest, Daniel was still searching for her, and he knew where she lived in Edmonton. If he didn't track her in the forest, he could always go after her back at the apartment. Until he was caught, she simply couldn't go back home. It was no longer an option.

But she certainly couldn't stay here. She was a liability, and she'd dragged these poor old folks into her situation. There was a man out there with a gun, and she'd basically brought his danger to their doorstep. If she couldn't go back to her home, what was she supposed to do? Stay here? Threaten these nice people's lives?

At this point, Emily determined, anybody who got close to her was in danger.

At the very least, they were probably trying to figure out what to do with her now that she was safely behind the bathroom door. Perhaps they would decide to call the police behind her back.

Emily reached over and turned off the shower water, finally feeling clean for the first time in hours. All things considered, after everything she felt wash away, she wouldn't mind having the police come around. But not for all the wrong reasons.

She knew she had to tell them.

Stepping out of the shower, she used the towel that Mary had provided for her to wipe herself dry and then made a move for her bloody clothes. But before she could reach them, she heard Mary on the other side of the door.

"Hello, miss?" Mary called through the door. "I went through the closet and found some old sweatpants and sweatshirts that I thought would fit you. I'm going to leave them by the door. Don't worry, Ollie's downstairs, and I'm going to go down to join him. Just change when you're ready. No reason for you to walk around in those bloody rags."

It didn't occur to Emily that Mary would go the extra mile

and find her something nice to wear. *This is too much*, she thought.

It was really going to hurt letting them down, she mused with a sinking feeling.

Reaching around the door and grabbing the clothes, she put them on. They felt ridiculously clean, and they were the nicest clothes she'd ever worn in her life, so comfortable, as if they were washed for her by her own grandmother. She went through the pockets of her jeans and pulled out her keys, phone, and earbuds, shoving them into the pockets of the sweatpants, and then stepped out, going back down the stairs to find the elderly couple sitting at the kitchen table.

As she approached, Ollie stood up, gave a polite little nod and bow, and then sat back down.

Mary poured water into a glass, setting it in front of Emily, and then passed over a bowl full of fruit. "I wasn't sure if you had any allergies or anything," she said warmly, "and I don't know if you've had anything before . . . well, before whatever happened to you, so I thought you might like this. I hope it's all right."

Emily could almost feel the fructose tempting her mouth, and she wondered if she was drooling. She immediately grabbed some strawberries and several blueberries before sitting down at the table and taking another gulp of water. The berries tasted delicious, and the water flooded her throat and stomach, making her feel as if she were experiencing water for the first time again.

Everything about these people was just wonderful.

"You know"—Ollie finally spoke up—"I've rarely seen people dive into a bowl of strawberries like you are. All things considered, you must've been through hell and back."

Emily continued to eat some grapes as she decided that there was no other time for her to say this, no reason to put any of this off. "You could certainly say that," she said in between swallowing fruit.

"Is your car up the road somewhere?" asked Ollie. "Do you need to call the towing service?"

"I don't have a . . . well, no, that's not true. I do have a car. But it's in Legal."

"Legal?" Mary asked, surprised. "You got in a car crash and walked all the way here from Legal?"

"I think there's been a misunderstanding. I didn't get into a car crash. I'm sorry for worrying you. And I'm sorry for waking you up."

"You didn't wake us up," said Ollie, smiling. "We're farmers. We're always up at this hour to do the chores and milk the cows."

"What do you mean you weren't in an accident?" said Mary, looking curious. "You look like you've been through quite a bit. And I don't just mean your clothes. I mean, well, just looking at you, your face and arms, you look like there was quite a lot going on."

"Well, yes, but it was something else. I was . . . well, I mean, I don't really know how to describe it so it makes sense. But I was attacked."

"My God!" Mary gasped. "By a wolf?"

Emily shook her head. She really needed to get this story out. "It was a person."

"Could've fooled us," said Ollie. "Sure looks like a bear was involved."

"Ollie!" snapped Mary. "Ignore him," she told Emily. "What do you mean you were attacked by a person? Somebody did this to you?"

"Yes. This all started last night when I went to a bar in Legal because . . . well, I found out that my boyfriend was . . . cheating on me. You know what, that just gets complicated. The point is, I went up there to end things with him, and along the way, some creep at the same bar decided to hit on me and wasn't really taking no for an answer. And since then, he refused to let it go."

"What do you mean he 'refused' to let it go?" asked Ollie, becoming angry and shocked.

"Well, I'm pretty sure he sabotaged my car, and then he spent the better part of the night chasing me as I tried to walk back to Edmonton, constantly hounding me and assaulting me. He even pulled a gun on me and shot at me."

Mary looked horrified. Emily hated putting that look on her face.

"My God," Mary said, covering her gaping mouth with her hand. "And you say you've never met this person before?"

"Well, I've never met him personally, but during all of this, he let me know that he's been following me for quite some time now. So apparently, I've had a stalker for who knows how long, and he didn't appreciate being told no."

"Where I come from," Ollie said, still looking furious but sounding composed, "a guy tries to do that to a young woman, all the other guys in town would round up and see him about a 'private matter' in his own living room. And see to it he wouldn't be able to walk out of that living room for a couple of weeks at least."

"Oh, lay off!" Mary snapped. "The police would round you up the moment they found out."

"I used to go to school with the local sheriff; remember Peter? Hell, he'd only arrest me if I forgot to invite him to the posse."

"Don't listen to him," Mary said reassuringly to Emily. "He hasn't had fun in forty years. Anyway, this man, he did this to you?"

Emily nodded. "Most of it. Of course, some of it is just from my running through the forest and falling down a cliff. But I think he's done a lot more than just hound me. As I walked, before I knew he was following me, I . . . I came across a car crash on the highway. And . . ."

The more she ran it through her head—the fact that it just happened to be her ex-boyfriend—the more it sounded to Emily like it was ridiculous.

"I found some people killed there. By gunshot, but they'd also been sliced up with a knife. You could see it on their bodies. And when this guy, the guy who's been attacking me, passed them by to follow me, he looked like he barely even noticed them. I'm not sure, but I'm worried he might have been involved."

"Do you have any proof of that?" asked Ollie.

"No. But I am also worried that maybe he was involved somehow in the cell towers and internet being down all over the area."

"Yes, we heard about that on the radio. Why do you think he's doing something with that as well?"

"Well, when he was coming after me in the forest, he was using a cell phone that worked. He still had service."

Mary said, "We don't have cell phones here, so we don't know much about those. Are you saying that it wouldn't have worked if the cell towers were down? It wouldn't have worked at all?"

"Well, I mean, you could still turn them on and maybe check the time or something. But if you needed anything that would require a signal to the outside world, like some sort of mapping or tracking service, he wouldn't have that. Except he did. So I have to wonder, was he already anticipating this? Especially given the fact that he told me he has been stalking me for weeks."

Emily looked up from her berries. Mary and Ollie were staring at her, shocked and dumbfounded. These people were so kind to her and had filled her belly with delicious fruit. She hated making them feel this way. "I'm sorry I brought this to you. I mean, I know how it must sound . . ."

"Well, like I said," he said, getting up from the table, "it sounds like you've been through hell and back. And you could either be completely honest with us, or you could be completely insane, but that doesn't change the fact that you need help after everything that's happened. Where I come from, you don't abandon the person who crawled bloody to your porch. We've got a landline here, and it's been working just fine. Mary, you go call Peter. I'll fetch the shotgun just in case this feller shows up looking for her."

"My God," Mary said, jumping from the table and going over to the telephone in the kitchen. "I haven't heard anything like this since that radio story about those poor women in West Edmonton! My God, people these days."

Emily sat there quietly, astounded. And relieved. They believed her. Or at least, they believed her so far as to immediately trust her enough to get her help.

She was actually going to be saved, she realized. Everything was going to be all right.

Ollie headed off to a set of stairs that led to some lower floor, probably a basement. She looked over at Mary as she picked up the landline phone and started pushing the buttons.

And then all the lights went out.

Somewhere in the darkness, Mary said, "The phone line is dead."

23

Emily didn't move. She was in a dark, unfamiliar house. And while she didn't have any proof of it, she felt confident that this was Daniel's doing. There had been, quite simply, far too much happening in her life for her to think it was anything, or anybody, else.

These people were kind to her, and she'd brought this to their doorstep.

In her panic, Emily realized that there was no reason for her to think that Daniel wasn't already in the house, and she shot upward, knocking the chair she was sitting on back as she flipped around, desperate to see if somebody was coming up on her in the dark.

She couldn't see anything clearly. She could only just make out the vague outline of doorways and pieces of furniture as her eyes began to adjust to the dark.

Stupidly, though, she'd created a lot of noise knocking over the chair, and both Mary and Ollie let out cries of surprise.

"Oh, my God!" Mary yelled.

"What happened?" Ollie called out from the basement stairs. "Is anybody hurt? What happened to all the lights?"

"Oh, what do you think happened, you idiot," Mary called out. "It's a power outage."

"Damn government," Ollie murmured. "Is everybody okay? I heard somebody fall over."

"That was my chair," Emily said, hearing the panic in her own voice. "I think it's that guy. I think he caused it."

"Let's not start up hysteria just yet," Mary said, hanging up the phone. "It could actually just be a bad fuse. Ollie, could you go down to the fuse box and take a look at it?"

"With what, my magic night-vision goggles? Sure, I'll just waltz down the dark steps and break my neck going down there. I'm sure you'd love that."

"Well, then get a flashlight or something. It's not like you haven't done this a million times before. You could find the fuse box blindfolded."

"So could you. Why don't you go find it, then?"

"I'm busy," she cried before picking the phone up again and trying to talk into it, as if that would fix it.

Emily knew it wouldn't be fixed. She knew that the guy who shut down the cell towers in the region would be able to handle an electronic matter like cutting phone lines. Or the power.

This is really happening, she thought. And it was her fault.

"I really think it was him," she said, trembling. "I think we need to . . ."

And then she didn't know how to finish that statement. What was she supposed to do now? Recommend they call the cops? Mary was just about to, and the phone line had been cut. These people didn't have cell phones. They had no other way of contacting the outside world.

Daniel was in complete control.

"What's the nearest town?" Emily said rapidly. "We could go to the police there."

"Closest place is Excelsior," Mary said, hanging up the phone again. "But that's just a little place where people gather. I mean, there's a gas station and a grocery store, but that's about it. Sheriff's office is all the way in Morinville. At this point, you'd probably be closer going all the way to Edmonton. Especially at this hour, Peter isn't known for being easy to wake up."

Emily's eyes further adjusted to the dark. She could make out the shapes of everything that she saw coming in, including the windows along the walls. She wondered where the fuse box was or where the phone line would've been for Daniel to cut it. She wondered which window he would break through first. She wondered when the bullets would start flying.

"Oh, God," she said, almost going hysterical. "God, how can you be calm like this?"

Emily almost jumped out of her skin as she felt a pair of hands come up on her shoulders until she realized that Mary had crossed the kitchen and was patting her gently, trying to calm her.

"Don't you worry, dear," she said. "There's always some junkie out of Edmonton sneaking up here, trying to find out if we grow marijuana or something. Wouldn't be the first time we've dealt with an emergency situation. But more than likely, it's just a bad power line, happens all the time. We'll get it fixed, and we'll—"

"I'm telling you, he's here!" Emily cried out. She could feel it happening again. She didn't want all of this to start up again.

She glanced at the basement stairs, and she could see a light floating around.

"No, all the fuses look fine," Ollie called up. "Maybe some animal started biting into—"

He never finished his sentence. There was a loud banging on the door. It wasn't the sound of anybody knocking on it. It sounded like somebody trying to kick it open.

Followed by the sound of somebody falling over and grunting.

Emily definitely heard it that time. And from the stiffness in Mary's hands, she knew Mary heard it too.

"Kill the light, Ollie," Mary said, sternly and with purpose.

Down in the basement, Ollie's flashlight turned off.

Emily heard Ollie fidgeting around, going through stuff, until she heard the unmistakable sound of him cocking a shotgun. In the dark, she could barely make out the outline of Mary marching over to the kitchen counter and pulling out a pair of sharp-looking knives.

Emily just stood there. She was woefully unprepared. But these people certainly weren't.

The front door was vibrating as it repeatedly got hit. She could feel Mary come back to her, now armed with a few blades, and heard Ollie come up the steps, armed with a very large shotgun.

By the time they were in a group again, the banging on the door stopped.

"He'll try the windows next," said Ollie.

"How do you know?" Emily asked.

"How else would he get in?"

"No, I mean, how do you know he won't try the door again? I mean, can he actually get through it?"

"Bulldozer couldn't get through it. This whole place is built to withstand a hurricane. Keeps us warm in the winter, keeps the dust out whenever a storm blows over. Nothing gets through that door unless I open it."

"But can he get through the windows?"

"No. Same story as the door. They're designed to withstand a building flying off the ground and crashing into them. No idiot junkie coming over from Edmonton is going to be able to bash one of those in."

"This isn't an idiot junkie from Edmonton."

"Doesn't scare me all the same."

Emily could tell from the sound of his voice that he meant it. This was a man who could face down a bear, and he still sounded like he could joke about it. This man was ready.

"You've got, uh, bullets in that shotgun?"

"You mean shells, dear," Mary corrected.

"And no," Ollie replied. "I'm not inclined to go killing anybody if I don't have to. It's just buckshot. Good for scaring off coyotes and the occasional meth head."

Emily wished it were a shell. She wished it were strong enough to kill. But she didn't say that out loud. She already hated that she was so quick to jump to murder, but she didn't want these people to think the same of her.

Though, the way they were talking about all this, Emily wondered if they would actually care about what she said.

Everything was quiet for a moment until they heard Daniel's voice—to Emily, the unmistakable voice of Daniel—tauntingly humming in the night. "Ha-ha-ha-ha," he said in a singsong voice.

Emily knew exactly where he was positioned. After apparently giving up on trying to break through the door, he was rounding the house, trying to find a weak window. He had just passed their back corner, probably rounding toward the windows facing west, out of the living room.

Mary went over to those windows.

"Where is she going?" Emily asked, worried about her benefactor's life. "What are you doing?"

Mary quickly turned back to Emily. "Quiet," she whispered as she gingerly tiptoed through the dark toward the back windows. She stood by one of the larger windows and then just stood there. And waited.

Mary was illuminated against the bright night sky, and Emily could see that she was still holding her knives, like fear's daggers ready to come down upon an opponent. She was gripping them like she was ready to strike.

And then Emily quietly gasped. She noticed Daniel coming into sight of the window.

He was now wearing a black ski mask. It was hard to make out the features of his face, but she knew it was him. After everything she'd been through, she had almost memorized the shape of that head, the height of that frame, its bulky girth.

He came up to the window. And when he saw that there was somebody standing there, he suddenly jumped back. Startled.

Looking up into the face of Mary, he stood frozen, like a deer in headlights. Suddenly, he ran back the way he came.

"Fucking little prick," Mary spat under her breath.

Emily wasn't expecting that. She wasn't expecting that kind of language to come from a lady so small and sweet.

She could hear the wrestling of bits of outdoor furniture and gravel as Daniel ran around to the front of the house. She also heard Mary leave her position and gingerly trot over to the front room, where there were more windows. Emily just stood, watching the events unfold. Ollie stood next to her, still gripping his gun. He hadn't moved an inch from his spot. If anything, it almost felt as if he was starting to sway, possibly bouncing from one heel to the next, trying to stave off the boredom.

Emily figured that he must have complete faith in his wife.

Emily watched as Mary arrived at the front and waited at

the window. She could just barely see Daniel slowly looking over, trying to peer in, before seeing Mary again and running off like a scared child to try to find another opening on the south side of the house.

"Usually happens this way," Mary muttered before following him around the house.

Emily couldn't believe how comfortably everything was going. She actually felt protected for the first time this entire evening.

Finally, she could see the dark frame of Daniel coming around the house, lumbering along the windows facing west as he arrived at the living room window, which he stared at once more. Mary caught up to him, knives in hand. This time, though, Daniel obviously took a different approach. Emily could see, even in the darkness, that he slowly pulled out his revolver and pointed it in her direction, threatening her.

Mary didn't move. She couldn't give a damn.

Daniel tapped the barrel of his gun against the window, trying to make her see that it was clearly there.

Mary almost looked bored.

Emily started to wonder how many times these two must have had a gun pointed in their faces. She wondered what kind of people she had found in the middle of the night. The kind of people who could face off with a murderer and not even blink.

Finally, realizing his tactics weren't working, Daniel pointed his gun at Mary, through the window, and fired off a bullet. The outside surface of the window grew cobwebs of white as the glass became damaged from the shot. But even from here, Emily could see that the rest of the window remained intact. It had barely suffered any damage at all. These people were absolutely right. This house was designed to withstand a hurricane.

After shooting it, Daniel hit the glass with the grip of his gun, only to be startled when the whole thing bounced off, causing no damage to the window. He hit it again.

This time, it was Mary's turn to hold up her knife to the window threateningly. She wanted Daniel to know that she was in complete control of the situation.

Emily watched as Daniel stepped off to the side and suddenly shook the wall. Evidently, he was trying to see if he could break through the architecture, maybe punch a hole through and climb in that way.

But the worst he did was shake anything attached to the wall. The rest of the house stood intact.

She also heard Daniel shriek and grumble, as if he had just hurt his hand, and he shouted many expletives afterward.

Emily knew that she was still trapped in the house with a killer surrounding them. But for the time being, this actually felt like it was going to work.

For however long it lasted.

24

Whatever Ollie and Mary might have thought of Emily before, she felt confident that they now believed that what she'd said about her attacker was true.

It was hard to deny that her situation was exactly as she'd described. After all, they now had their own personal experience to go by.

They were locked inside their own house, which had its power lines cut, as well as its phone line. And they were being stalked by a man wearing black tactical gear to blend into the night and carrying a revolver.

This wasn't a run-of-the-mill criminal that Mary and Ollie had dealt with in the past. They talked frequently about how they had dealt with people of this caliber before. But this was different. This was a man who came prepared with the kind of clothes that were necessary for being able to move without detection in the night. He had already planned this long ahead and was prepared for dealing with an assault situation. He also came equipped with weaponry. Granted, none of it worked, but nevertheless, Mary and Ollie had largely dealt with random people who decided to commit crimes far outside the city, hoping—without any plausibility—that they would be able to escape the law out here. According to them, it was usually just people desperate enough to travel out this far in the hope of finding drugs or maybe even weapons. They were usually in for a surprise.

The fact that Daniel certainly got a rude awakening didn't change the fact that he also came out here with intent. This was different.

On top of that, previous attackers to the property wouldn't have come, according to Mary, with the ability to cut the power lines. Most of them wouldn't even know where the power lines were located leading out of the house or wouldn't have the tools or the capability to cut them safely without injuring themselves. Mary told her that in the entire time they'd lived in this house, nobody went out of their way to cut the lines illegally. It just never happened.

Not until tonight, Emily thought.

Not until she entered their lives.

So now, quite assuredly, Mary and Ollie were trapped in their house by a person who had the skills and the means to carry out a vicious assault. Even though the connection was circumstantial, Emily knew that it wouldn't be that much of a leap of the imagination to assume that a person who was willing to do this would also be capable of destroying cell towers for an entire area. He would also be able to cut the fuel line in a car. He was certainly the person who would be willing to put in the effort to chase a woman across several counties for an entire night. Everything that Emily had told the couple had been the truth.

She'd brought this to their house. It was her fault.

After the escapade where Daniel struggled to get inside the house, and probably injured his hand in the process, he continued to loop around the house to find a way in. He kept banging on several windows and struggled to punch—or maybe, at that point, ram his shoulder—into the walls, hoping there was a weak point that he could break through. It started to become a little pathetic and sad after a while.

Emily was following his presence around the house, but after a while, she felt confident that he simply wouldn't get in. Her eyes drifted back to the one part of the window that he'd tried to shoot out with a bullet. "Are you sure that he won't be able to do that again?" she asked. "I mean, that window looks kind of damaged. What if he, I don't know, shoots it twice or something?"

"Couple of years back," Ollie said, "old Travis McIntyre got drunk and decided to come over to play cards. He drove his car into the side of our house. Straight into a window. Whole thing was scratched up on the outside, but it still held. So even if this feller decided to get himself a car and try to do the same thing, it will still hold. I promise you, the outside of the glass is going to need some repairs to make it look nice and clear again. But it should hold. They're all like that."

"Maybe if we're lucky"—Mary spoke up—"he'll be stupid enough to try it again, and it might actually ricochet and hit the guy."

Emily turned to her. "Wait, can that actually happen?"

"No," Ollie said. "Bullets don't ricochet off the glass that way. The glass absorbs the shot, and the bullet falls to the ground. It's just wishful thinking. Can't blame her. It's a nice idea."

Almost at the perfect moment, they did hear another gunshot, followed by some bashing. It was coming from the basement.

Ollie, with the shotgun firmly in his hands, went marching down to the basement. Mary stayed above with Emily and waited for him to return. They didn't have to wait long, as he was back up barely half a minute later.

"Tried to do the same thing with the basement window," he said. "Saw me, and he ran off. I think he knows I have a shotgun now."

And with that, nobody spoke for the next few minutes. By which point, no matter how strong their resolve, everyone in the house looked at each other and came to the same conclusion. Daniel didn't know what to do, so he stopped trying to break in. He had backed off.

They had no reason to believe that he had just given up and left, of course. Emily knew him too well by this point, and the couple seemed very realistic about what an attacker would be willing to do. But all things considered, they started moving off in different directions.

Emily didn't know what was happening until Mary grabbed her by the wrist and pulled her along upstairs. "You'd better come with me, dearie," she said. "Not a good idea to be leaving you alone at the moment."

"Why?" asked Emily. "Where are we going?"

"To check all the other windows and means of entrance," Mary replied. "They're all as strong and as secure as the other ones, but there's always the possibility that we didn't think of something. Or maybe something got worn with time, or maybe he might get it through his head to come in through the roof, which actually isn't as secure as the rest of the house, though nobody actually knows that. Still, it would be irresponsible not to check. Ollie's checking all the windows downstairs."

"Do you want me to help you check?"

Mary was silent for a moment before responding, "To be honest, child, I couldn't imagine how I would feel if I knew I left you alone in the house, and that man ended up finding a way in here anyway. I'm not really a movie watcher, but even I know you shouldn't split up people in a situation like this."

"Well, by that logic, shouldn't we still be with Ollie?"

Mary started checking the windows in the various upstairs rooms, looking through the master bedroom. "Ollie is, well, many things. But if there's one thing I can say about him that I would rather he never hear me say, it's that I can always count on him to do the right thing when it's a matter of life or death."

"That sounds great, Mary. Why wouldn't you want to tell him that?"

Mary turned to Emily and smiled. "When you're with somebody for this long, it's a good idea not to start giving them a big head. Might start getting ideas."

Emily smiled back. It was the first time she remembered smiling all night.

It was amazing to think that this couple seemed to be having a good time out of all of this, or, at least, as much of a good time as possible under the circumstances. They must've been married for decades by now and knew each other's idiosyncrasies. They were even playfully mean to each other in a way that seemed very endearing in her mind. It was amazing to Emily that a couple could last this long and still find a way to have fun.

As Mary stepped out of her bedroom, securing the thought that those windows were fine, she walked down the upstairs hallway to the window at the opposite end. She checked how secure it was and also stopped to look around outside, probably to see if Daniel was skulking around somewhere. On the way over, she passed by the door to the bathroom.

Emily remembered that it had one of those little upper windows in it, probably to allow natural sunlight in the daytime, without being large or low enough for any peeping toms to be able to see through. Emily looked inside, hoping to be helpful by checking this window as well.

In the dark of night, she really couldn't tell. And frankly, she knew that she didn't have the skill to be able to check up on home renovations or the quality of windowpanes. All she could see was the shower where Mary had allowed her to get cleaned up.

And now this nice couple was in danger.

"I'm so sorry," she finally said to Mary.

"What's that?"

"I'm so sorry for bringing this to you. For ruining your life. You probably weren't expecting any of this. I really shouldn't have . . ."

Mary walked over and grabbed onto Emily's hand. "It's a harsh world. Some people are poor and starving. Some people are drug addicted in the big city, coming out here to harass farmers. Some women get killed over on the west side and thrown into a dumpster. Some people, like you, get harmed. Some people like me and Ollie could get harmed. It could happen to anybody. It could happen anytime. But the last thing you can allow it to ever do, as I've discovered in my long, long life, is to allow any of it to give you a reason to give up on looking forward. The moment you let people make the decision for you to just up and quit on life is the moment that you effectively let them beat you anyway, even if they never got a chance to take your life away the old-fashioned way. You still let them find a way. And I say don't let them. If you hadn't shown up here tonight, you'd probably still be out there and very possibly dead. And maybe this Daniel person would've attacked us anyway, for all I know. At least this way, we'll be fine, and you'll be fine."

"Thank you, Mary." There was so much more that Emily wanted to say to her new friend but would never get the chance, as they started hearing a horrible rumbling coming from downstairs.

Both of them immediately ran down the stairs as fast as they could.

They met up with Ollie, who had a shotgun trained on the front door.

"Ollie, what's happening?" Mary asked.

"Bastard must've gotten to my power tools in the shed," said Ollie, aiming his gun fiercely at the door. "Must've found the industrial-strength stuff, because he started up my buzz saw, and he's coming at the frame of the door."

"Can he get through?" asked Emily. "I thought you said this thing could handle a hurricane."

"The door? Yes. The frame? Yes. And if it were a hurricane, then it wouldn't be able to separate the door from the frame because it's too tight, and a hurricane is just a bunch of wind anyway. But a human being? A person will probably figure out that the hinges, even though they're metal, are probably the weakest points. Sure, they can stand up to a hurricane, but if he got a strong enough saw, he probably figured out that that's the place to hit it."

And sure enough, Emily watched as glowing sparks emanated from between the door and the frame. First on the top, and then on the bottom.

"You ladies might wanna step back," said Ollie.

The two women complied.

Once the sparks ended and the buzzing stopped, there was a loud bang, and the door shook loose from its frame. Another loud bang, and the door slid out and fell over.

And Daniel stepped over the threshold. "Come out, come out, wherever you—"

And then the idiot never quite got to finish his taunting as Ollie immediately fired off a hail of buckshot at him.

Daniel fell over sideways as his left arm flailed backward, evidently getting hit in the shoulder.

Apparently, Emily realized, the idiot had decided to take a moment to mock Emily instead of immediately expecting a dangerous situation. His loss, really.

Falling over on the door frame, Daniel pulled up his firing arm. Righting himself and standing back up, he fired off a pair of shots from his revolver.

Ollie dove over to the right, while cocking his shotgun, and fired off his second buckshot volley.

This time, the shot hit Daniel square in the chest and lifted him off his feet, sending him flying back out the door he came through.

Emily watched to see if Daniel would get back up, but her attention veered away when Mary, in a mad rush, jumped down to Ollie on the ground.

She was tending to her husband's wound. Ollie was clutching his shoulder. Even in the dark, Emily could smell the iron. He had been shot through the shoulder and was losing blood fast.

Once Emily got to her knees, she took a look at his shoulder, which she could now see was bleeding heavily.

When Mary realized that Emily was now caring for her husband's shoulder, she immediately grabbed the shotgun and opened it, ready to reload. She stopped when an engine roared in the driveway.

Running up to the door and finishing her reload, Mary watched as an SUV—Emily figured, the couple's SUV—drove off in the night. Daniel must've hot-wired it and stolen their vehicle.

They were safe for the moment. Their attacker was gone.

Emily didn't know what to do except apply pressure. Somewhere, in her meandering life of bad college degrees and worse boyfriends, she had never developed survival skills like basic first aid. She figured that the kind of injury that Ollie sustained would require a tourniquet, but she didn't know how to create one or where to apply it. She didn't even know if that was the appropriate recommendation under the circumstances. All she knew was that when she was bleeding, holding her finger down on the part where she bled would usually stop the flow.

She pressed her whole hand into Ollie's shoulder. The old man gritted his teeth and grimaced in pain. Emily could feel the blood flowing over her hands. She didn't think it was stopping the bleeding.

And there was more blood everywhere.

25

"Mary," Emily called out frantically, "what do I do? It won't stop bleeding!"

"Well, that's a good start," Mary replied, coming back to the two of them. "Keep applying pressure. Here's a clean rag to hold there to help stop the flow. Ollie, do you know if it was a clean shot?"

"I think it was," the old man said, breathing hard. "But still hurts like hell. I think he hit a bone or something."

"Oh, walk it off, you big baby. And while you're at it, walk to the van. We got to get you to a hospital."

"Wait, you have another vehicle? A van?"

"Yes, the minivan. It just sits in the garage since we got the SUV. It's been pretty useless."

"Not that useless," said Ollie, lifting himself to his feet and using his wife for support. "I always liked the minivan. You can get all your friends in there."

Mary carried the brunt of her husband's weight over her shoulders as she walked him toward the door that led to the garage. "At your age, you need fewer drinking buddies."

"Don't you sass me, woman."

"Ollie, we've got cows that weigh less than you do right now. Now shut up and get in the van."

Emily carried the shotgun—an object she had no idea how to handle—as gingerly as possible as she followed the couple into the garage. Standing there a minivan perfectly suited for an adorable little family.

She waited for Mary to pull out a pair of keys and press the button to unlock everything. She then opened the back door of the van and carefully placed her husband into it, pushing down the backseats in order to give him more room to lie down. "Now keep that compress on there, Ollie," she said and then gestured to the front passenger door. "Go on and climb in there, dear."

Once they were all in, Mary pressed a little electronic button on the visor above her seat, and Emily watched as the garage door automatically opened. Mary started the car and quickly backed out, then hit the button again, closing the door. She backed down the driveway, right onto the highway, and headed south.

"Where are we going?" asked Emily.

"Royal Alexandra. Closest hospital."

Emily was familiar with it. The Royal Alexandra Hospital was the central hospital in downtown Edmonton. After everything that had happened, she was finally getting a ride back to her hometown. It was sad that it had to happen under the worst of possible circumstances.

She didn't think she could live with herself if after all was said and done, another human being ended up dying for her. She didn't want Ollie to die.

She didn't want to be responsible for any more suffering.

Emily watched as the van sped down the highway. The roads were still empty, but looking farther out, they got to a point where Emily could see the city lights on the horizon, beginning to inch into view. She knew it wouldn't be long before they would reach the outskirts of town, where the residents would be heading off to work in the city, and the various other employees would be doing their early morning drives to get to their early shifts at all the city shops. It wouldn't be long now, Emily figured, before she would return to civilization, of the urban variety that she was used to, and see the thriving city take up the roads. She would finally be surrounded by people again. Normal people who just wanted to leave her alone.

In the meantime, though, Emily focused on the people at hand. Looking over at Mary, Emily didn't have the words to express to her just how sorry she was that all of this had escalated so far and gotten her husband injured in the process. All the same, Emily figured that Mary wasn't really interested in hearing it right now, anyway. She had a look of fierce determination in her eyes, focusing on the road, making sure that she was able to drive quickly and safely to the hospital downtown, to get her husband to a surgeon. Emily felt that she understood, looking on it now. It was similar to the look Mary had had when Daniel was stalking the outside of their house. But at the same time, Emily could just barely see the faintest twinkle of a glow in the tears in her eyes.

Mary was genuinely scared that something would happen to her husband. That she was going to lose him.

Emily couldn't even begin to imagine what she could say to Mary that would fix any of this.

Turning away instead, she looked behind her at Ollie lying on the backseat of the minivan. Emily didn't know if this was in any way more beneficial than sitting upright, but for what it was worth, it was Mary's idea to lay her husband in the back of the van. And Ollie seemed rather comfortable with the whole notion of it. It was the position that seemed to put him at ease, and he did appear to be breathing easier. Briefly, while Emily was looking at him, Ollie opened his eyes and gave her a little smile and a wink, probably his way to let her know that he was going to be okay.

She smiled back, but it didn't help. She was still very concerned.

In the rearview behind their car, Emily could see that they had just passed an intersection that led to some houses in the middle of nowhere. Probably the northernmost houses in Edmonton, built on the outskirts in the city's continuing urban expansion into surrounding territory. Then another field, and soon, they passed by another intersection, this one leading into some sort of gated community. A car drove out of this intersection and turned in the same direction, heading south.

It was the first car Emily had seen all night that felt "normal" to her. It was the first time she felt like she was back home.

Breathing another sigh of relief, she leaned back in her seat.

"What happened?" Mary asked, for the first time revealing a certain amount of panic in her voice. "Is everything okay?"

"Ollie looks like he's doing fine," Emily replied. "And it's just nice to be back home again. I just feel like . . . feel like—"

Emily was about to add that she felt like everything was back to normal but stopped short as something in the passenger-side mirror caught her eye.

She looked back behind her, past Ollie, out the back window of the van. Behind them were a few cars. They were traveling along at the same speed Mary was driving, fairly normally. However, one SUV was driving especially fast.

And straight at them.

"It's him!" Emily screamed. "Daniel must have recognized us. He's back! He's going to ram us!"

26

Emily braced herself as the SUV bashed the back of their van.

Mary floored it and put some distance between them and the SUV, but not much before Daniel evidently added gas and moved to catch up with them.

All of a sudden, the SUV spun to the left and caught up with another, smaller car that the minivan was speeding past. With brute force, the SUV slammed into the little car and forced it to collide with the back of the van.

"Shit!" Mary shouted.

The collision almost caused a pit maneuver and would've flipped the van over sideways if Mary didn't expertly steer the car away and drive into oncoming traffic instead. Emily grabbed the dash and braced herself for the worst as Mary swerved around a few honking, desperate cars before she drove back onto her side of the road.

The van continued to speed as fast as it could go as the SUV wound around the accident it had caused and closed the gap between itself and the van. Suddenly, the back window shattered as it was struck with a bullet, making Emily and Mary duck in their seats.

Ollie started to sit up, but Mary cried out, "Ollie, keep your ass down! For God's sake!"

Another shot rang out, and Emily cringed as the bullet ricocheted off the ceiling of the car and hit the windshield up front, damaging the glass directly in front of her face.

The bastard was shooting at them while driving. "Emily, pass me the gun," Ollie ordered, extending his good arm toward Emily.

"You can barely sit up straight!" Mary yelled. "Emily, can you drive while I—"

Emily had no interest in driving the van. She was tired of being helpless in all of this. Also, she wasn't sure how easily she would be able to switch into the driver's seat while they were still in motion.

But she figured she could understand the basic concept of the gun.

Emily picked up the shotgun and crawled to the back of the van.

Pointing the barrel out the shattered window, she aimed it vaguely in the direction of the SUV and fired off a shot. It seemed to send a scattering of buckshot wildly behind them, possibly not even hitting the car. Emily kept pulling her finger against the trigger and couldn't understand why nothing was happening until she remembered she needed to cock the shotgun.

Emily lined up her shot, but before she could pull the trigger, she felt another bullet from Daniel whiz past her hair. This time, Emily used the van window to help point the barrel and keep it steady. Emily fired, and the buckshot sprayed the front grille of the SUV. It appeared to do much more damage than hitting the windshield, as smoke started to billow out from the front of the SUV.

"Pass that thing over to me," Ollie said. "I'll reload it."

"Just show me how to do it," Emily cried.

But it was a moot point all the same. They never did get a chance to reload the gun.

Shortly after the second shot, Emily watched as the SUV slowed down. It made a sharp right, steering away from the action.

At first, Emily wondered if this was part of some new strategy and if Daniel was genuinely a step ahead of them, already knowing what would come next.

And in a way, that was exactly what it was, Emily soon realized. Blue and red lights started flashing as a police car blared its siren and started following the van.

Emily had been anticipating something like this for the entire evening. Not exactly this situation. After all, she was crouching down in the back of the van next to a dying man while holding a gun. She certainly wasn't expecting to be pulled over by the police in this capacity.

Now she was staring out the back window of Mary's van, watching the lights of a police car spin while its siren continued to blare. The police were really here.

And although she'd spent the entire night thinking about what was going to happen, now that it was right in front of her, she was astounded that it was really happening.

Her entire body ran cold, probably for the hundredth time that night. She could feel her head shaking. Her eyes felt bloodshot, and she felt her mind both going blank and being flooded with a headache. It was the overwhelming response of police presence that affected her. She stared at all of this right in front of her and wondered, why me, why me?

She honestly had no idea what was going to happen to her, or to the lot of them, now that the police were here.

Casually glancing sideways, she saw the end of the barrel of Ollie's shotgun, still held in her hands, still vaguely pointing out the window. Now somewhat in the direction of the police.

She immediately realized that this was not at all a good look. She threw the gun down to the floor of the van.

Which seemed to have been enough to offend the police. Before, while she was still holding the gun, they only periodically started up their siren, probably just to warn the speeding van that it should pull over. Now, though, they turned it on and left it on. It was the loudest thing in the entire city that early morning.

The police probably just spotted her pointing a shotgun at them. She had no idea what that was going to result in, but at this point, Emily was willing to just add it to the list. Her long, long list of incidents from this nightmare.

"Well," said Ollie weakly, "I guess that explains why the shooting stopped." He snickered and started coughing a little. He smiled, even as he closed his eyes and rested his head, still breathing, but shallowly.

Emily admired the fact that he still had enough strength to try to joke his way out of this. But both she and Mary understood that he was probably on his last legs at this point. The gunshot wound was affecting him far more seriously than he let on.

For the first time in as long as she could remember, Emily had met the nicest man she had ever known. She wished there were more men in the world like Ollie. She certainly didn't want to lose the only one she'd met.

At the same time, the police were here. They couldn't just flee from the scene.

As the noise and the lights continued to fill the night, Emily crawled back up to the passenger seat and looked at Mary. "We'd better pull over."

"When we get to the hospital, sure," Mary replied.

Emily did a double take and stared at Mary, wondering if

she'd heard right. "We're still a couple of miles away from the Royal Alexandra. We can't just drive there with the police following us the whole time."

"Says who?" asked Mary.

Emily had no idea where this night was going anymore. Not that she ever really did, all things considered.

"Mary," Emily finally said, more loudly and sternly, "they want us to pull over. I mean, what are we supposed to do? Just keep going?"

"That is exactly what I'm going to do," Mary said, far more calmly than she should be with everything going on in her life right now. "I'm going to drive this van straight to the hospital, and I'm going to drop off my dying husband in the emergency room so they can save his life. And I'm going to tell the police, when they finally catch up with us, that was my motivation and exactly what I was willing to do. And if it offends them that I disregarded their fucking authority, then they can either discuss it with me or kiss my ass because I have no intention of following the technicality of a bylaw while letting my husband die. And if they continue having a problem with this, I would be more than happy to discuss it with them after I pound their faces into the pavement. Does that sound all right to you?"

Emily stayed quiet. She suspected it was a rhetorical question.

"You'd better listen to her, dear," Ollie called out, still pretty weak. "It's usually not a good idea to argue with my wife about stuff like this. Never worked out for me."

Emily heard him and tried to laugh along with Ollie, but all she could hear was the last strength of his voice. He wasn't doing well.

She sat forward, staring at the road in front of her. *To hell with it*, she thought. This had already been a horrible night. She didn't want to lose a good man in the process. At this point, clearly, resisting arrest was probably going to be the least of her problems, she figured.

The major highway leading north out of Edmonton, in the opposite direction, simply merged with the major thruway street that ran through the center of the city. By this point, there were considerably more streetlights and road directions, but that was to be expected, along with all the local traffic of early birds simply trying to get to work. One of the advantages, Emily realized, of having a police car with a siren blaring behind them was that everybody assumed that the police car needed to get through and automatically moved out of the way of the van. They were even able to run every single red light without the slightest concern for collisions. They had a pretty straight and uneventful drive all the way to the Royal Alexandra Hospital. It probably helped Ollie a great deal.

Once they got to the hospital, Mary drove right up to the emergency door and leapt out of the van, running to the back door.

Several orderlies rushed out of the hospital with a gurney already prepared. Presumably, they had done this many times before in their life.

Emily ran around to the back and managed to catch up just as the police were exiting their cruiser.

"Is there any kind of assistance you need?" the first officer asked.

Emily stopped, frozen and taken aback. She was expecting considerably worse treatment from the police, considering they'd just evaded being pulled over for more than forty blocks. "We're sorry we didn't pull over," Emily awkwardly replied.

"We assumed something was wrong when you didn't pull over," the second officer replied. "But then we saw the van pull into the emergency hospital lane; well, it wasn't hard to figure out. Honestly, we figured a woman was delivering a baby or something."

Mary helped lift Ollie out of the back of the van and lugged him toward the gurney that had just appeared next to her. "Do I look pregnant to you?" she asked angrily.

Emily knew that Mary would not even be remotely concerned with decorum at the moment. And she, herself, really couldn't do much more for Ollie. It was time to face the music. It wasn't like the police were going to give her any more leeway.

"Thank you for escorting us," Emily started politely. "My name is Emily Corrigan. These people helped save my life. I was being chased by a horrible person all night. He tried to kill me on several occasions. He's been stalking me for weeks on end. And when I reached their house, these people took me in and protected me from him. They helped clean me up. But he attacked them, and Ollie got shot, so we needed to get him to the hospital. The man stole their SUV and tried to ram us off the road and was firing at us, so I used the shotgun, and I think I managed to damage the engine and make him back off. That's when you all discovered us. We're very sorry we didn't pull over. We were worried he was going to die."

"Thank you, we understand," the first officer replied. "It's unconventional, but under the circumstances, you made a pretty smart decision. But can you explain a little more? What were you saying? You were being chased by somebody tonight?"

"Yes. I was . . . see, I went to break up with my boyfriend, who was at a bar in Legal, when another bar patron tried to assault me, and I rejected him. When I got outside to my car, it wouldn't work, so I started walking. Since then, that man has been chasing me, harassing me, and terrorizing me. He revealed that he's been planning to come after me for quite some time now."

"When did this happen, exactly? And where?"

"I don't have the exact time, but I got to the bar just after sunset last night in Legal."

"And you weren't able to drive back? Or did your boyfriend drive you out there?"

"No, I drove myself, like I said, but my car wasn't working when I left the bar. I believe that Daniel, the man chasing me, damaged my car, preventing me from driving back, so I had to walk back on my own. I've been walking all night."

"So do you know the individual? The assailant?"

"No, I never met him before last night."

"Can you describe the individual?"

"Taller than me by about a foot. A little portly, a slight overbite, you could see some buckteeth. Disheveled looking, flat, oily hair. Physically strong—he has muscular, hairy hands. I don't know how else to describe him . . . kind of had the, you know, stereotypical office nerd look. If you know what I'm getting at."

The officers stopped asking questions and stared at her, their eyes widening a little bit. Until the first officer spoke up again. "You said his name is Daniel?"

"That's how he introduced himself to me, yeah. Why?"

The two police officers looked at each other knowingly. One of them turned and went back to the police car.

The other one stayed with Emily. "Well, it's just that this fits the description of another assailant."

"You already have this guy on file?"

"Not exactly. Just as a person of suspicion. Have you heard anything about the recent collection of murders out on the west side? Some women's bodies left in a dumpster?"

"Y-yeah, on the news last night. Why?"

"Some witnesses indicate that they saw a man fitting his description in that area," the officer shared. "He has been identified as a man named Daniel. I'm going to need you to look at a photo and tell me if this is the man who has been chasing and harassing you."

Emily nodded, swallowing hard. "Um, there's more. I think he murdered Jeremy and his other girlfriend . . . I, um, as I was walking, I came across his car on the side of the road. They'd been shot . . . and stabbed . . ." Emily was shaking as she mentioned this. "I touched—" She wrung her hands. "My phone wasn't working, and I wanted to call the police, so I . . ."

"It's okay, this man is dangerous. Just tell us if this is the same guy who has been chasing you all night." He took the photo from the other officer and showed it to her.

Emily stared at the image of her attacker. "Yes, that's him."

27

E mily sat in the waiting room at the Royal Alexandra Hospital. Emily had personally never been here before, as she'd never had a reason to visit the hospital. She was always very healthy and had never even broken a bone. Frankly, the injuries she'd received from running through the forest the entire evening were about the worst her flesh had ever experienced. A quick shower over at Mary's place had fixed that.

This was different, though. She really cared about Ollie. She didn't want to be the reason this man's long life suddenly came to an abrupt end. And she certainly didn't want Mary remembering her this way.

Of all the things that had happened to her, she certainly didn't want to be responsible for this. Not this.

She was sitting in the waiting room next to Mary, who was listening to the horrible things being told to her by the two officers standing before them. Emily was also listening in, but she couldn't take her eyes off the television screen. There wasn't any audio coming from the TV, but there was still a news tracker at the bottom of the report that was playing, so it wasn't hard to determine what was being shown.

The lead news report was that the third body in the case of the dead women found in a dumpster on the west side of town had finally been identified.

Natasha Flint, local real estate agent. Thirty years old upon death. The TV screen showed her face, from a photo probably downloaded from some social media site of hers. She was smiling with friends.

And right next to her, the graphics of the news report showed another face, the face of Daniel. Only here, he was identified as Daniel Powers and was listed as an electronic technician, age thirty-six. The photo they got of him looked like it was taken accidentally, as if somebody was taking a photo of somebody else and Daniel just happened to be in the background. He was walking alone. Sneering.

It seemed fitting, Emily thought. She turned from the TV and gave her full attention to the police.

"After forensics were able to identify the body of Miss Flint," one of the officers continued, "we began asking in the vicinity whether anybody had seen anything suspicious. Some colleagues of Miss Flint said that a car had been hanging around and followed her after she said she wanted to go out to celebrate a recent home sale, but she wanted to go somewhere her usual crowd wouldn't recognize her. Her friends haven't seen her since, obviously, but they did report that a dark sedan had been hanging around and followed her car as she drove away, at which point it wasn't seen in the neighborhood again. We ran a search on the license plate, and we got the information for a Daniel Powers."

The other officer addressed Emily. "We were going to look for him and question him, but you're saying that you encountered him earlier tonight?"

"Yes," said Emily. "He was just hanging around at a bar up

in Legal, where I went to confront my cheating boyfriend. I think he was prepared to find me there, because later in the night, he admitted that he's been stalking me for quite some time. He was able to chase me around after my car wouldn't start."

"And you say this was in Legal?"

"Yeah. Why?"

"After we identified the body, we started a search for her car. We recently got a report that a car matching Miss Flint's vehicle's description was found at a late night bar in that town."

"Seriously? That's where he got her?"

"We can't speak to that at the moment. There's a lot that we're still looking into in the area. Evidently, it's a pretty rough part of the region. A bartender was also assaulted sometime this evening as well."

Emily felt faint and tried not to look too nervous. "My goodness."

"So, getting back to your assailant, you said he was harassing you as you were walking down the highway?"

"Yes."

"Did he take any other aggressive action toward you?"

"He absolutely took aggressive action toward me. I am convinced that he murdered my ex-boyfriend and his lover somewhere down the road between here and Legal." She had told the other officer the same, but apparently, they wanted more details.

The officers looked at her briefly and wrote quickly on their digital pads. "What leads you to believe that?" the officer said.

"Because as I was walking down the road, I heard two gunshots, which I at first thought were tires blowing out on a car, but as I walked farther down the road, I noticed my ex-boyfriend's car on the side of the road, and I found him and his new girl, a woman named Erica, in the car. They'd been murdered."

"And did you make any attempt to call the police?"

"I made lots of attempts to call the police all the way down the highway. My phone didn't work."

"Yes, that's understandable, miss. The entire city and a few of the surrounding towns had blacked out cell and internet coverage. Things are starting to finally reconnect, though. We have an emergency tower set up in downtown Edmonton. But I imagine some of the farming regions will still be out for several days."

"Typical." Mary finally spoke up.

"And did you see the assailant, miss?" the officer said, turning to Mary.

"It's Mrs. And no, not at that time. When my husband found Emily here on our front porch, she looked like she had been assaulted and run through the wringer. We cleaned her up and fed her, but her assailant managed to track her down, and he attempted to assault us. He wasn't able to get into the house, but I saw him through the window. He was wearing some sort of black ski mask and black clothing. But all the other details about him match the physical description she gave. He was a little squat, a little portly, a little strong. I'd certainly recognize his voice and would be able to recognize it if I heard it again. He broke into my house and shot my husband. That's why we're here."

"We understand, ma'am, but you're telling us that you can't ID the perpetrator physically?"

"I never saw his face, no."

"Can you speak to the veracity of Miss Corrigan's story?"

"She showed up on my fucking porch covered in fucking blood and looking like death. Is that good enough for you?"

Emily tried to hide her smirk. She hoped that she would be able to get to an age when it would be socially acceptable for her to just officially no longer give a fuck, even in the face of the police. It sounded like it would be a pretty pleasant time.

As the policeman remained silent, apparently not knowing how to react to this rather stubborn old lady, behind them, an older police officer in a trench coat approached. She carried herself with a sense of professionalism and determination. Emily immediately determined that she was a higher-ranking officer. As it turned out, she was right.

"Good evening, ladies," she said professionally. "My name is Detective Cole, and I'm the investigator looking into the murders on the west side of town. Firstly, I'd like to say how grateful we are for your cooperation and how sorry we are about everything that's happened to you this evening. Secondly, we are very grateful, Miss Corrigan, for the information that you provided to us. Based on this information, we can start the search for Mr. Powers."

"Weren't you already looking for him?" asked Emily. "These guys said you ran his license plate through your search."

"It's true, we were looking for him as a person of interest, but now, knowing that his car was last seen in the area of the death of Miss Flint and that it crashed not too far from Excelsior, in addition to all your other accusations of his conduct this evening, we're able to upgrade it to a full warrant for his arrest."

"But will you be able to find him? I mean, he's very good at hiding. And tracking. And tech. I forgot to mention, he had a working phone during the outage. I think he may have had something to do with the outage itself . . . I mean, at least, I think so."

"We'll have every officer in the city out looking for him. We're doing everything we can."

"That's not good enough!" Emily suddenly burst out,

practically yelling. "This guy knows where I live. He's been there before. I can't go home now."

"Do you have anywhere else you can stay?"

"I don't think so. And I don't want anybody else getting in the way of . . . well, in the way of anybody coming after me."

Mary leaned over and put her hand on Emily's back. "Darling, if you really are worried, we can always bring you back to our home. I don't want you having to suffer through any more of this."

For the first time in a long time, Emily's body was filled with warmth.

"As another option"—the detective spoke up—"we can also put you up in a police safe house. You would be under guard, and we would be able to protect you. Given that you are now a witness, in regard to our search for Mr. Powers, we would prefer that you not leave the Edmonton region. For your safety."

Emily nodded. The truth was, she would've been very happy to have stayed with Mary again, but after everything she'd put them through, no matter how nice they were to her, she didn't have any interest in doing it all again. She had no intention of hurting them anymore.

The police detective was interrupted when the doctor came out and approached Mary. "Mrs. Ross?" he asked her. "Good evening, I'm Dr. Styles. I was operating on your husband tonight. I wanted to let you know that he's doing exceptionally well, and he's going to be just fine."

Mary practically collapsed onto Emily and gave her the biggest hug while silently crying. Emily hugged her back.

Detective Cole looked around at the officers and silently brushed them away. "I think we can finish this up later," she said, politely stepping away from the situation.

"He had bullet shrapnel lodged in the shoulder," the doctor continued, "but we were able to remove it quite easily.

We also sewed up the muscle damage he had experienced. There was some bone damage to his shoulder blade, but that will heal in time and with a good medical program. For the most part, he's recuperating from extreme blood loss and the shock of the operation. He's resting now, but if you'd like to see him, I would be happy to show you to the room."

Mary couldn't stop crying. She didn't say anything as she followed the doctor.

Emily followed them until she got to the emergency room door, where a nurse stopped her.

"And are you related to the family?" she asked Emily.

"Oh! Well, no."

"We're very sorry, family only at the moment."

Emily stopped in her tracks and just nodded. It was awkward, but she understood.

Evidently, so did Mary, as she turned, still crying, and gave Emily a warm smile and a friendly wave.

A second later, the doors closed, and Emily was alone in the waiting room.

She silently walked back to her seat and sat down, taking another moment to rest her weary legs, not knowing what else to do. She looked up at the television screen still reporting on the murders of those three women. She couldn't believe that Daniel was responsible for all these deaths and that she probably would've been the next one if things had turned out differently.

At first, she was disappointed in the police force's simply saying that after putting out a warrant for the arrest of Daniel, all they would do was look around for him. But the more she thought it through, the more she realized this was a better sign than she'd anticipated. After all, Daniel was still alive. And he was still hunting her.

And he was still in Edmonton. Where he knew she was as well. Meaning he wasn't going to leave anytime soon.

28

E mily didn't have much else to do at this point. She was exhausted and desperately wanted to sleep, but adrenaline kept pumping through her body. She knew that Daniel was still out there, somewhere, looking for her. And she also knew that until she ended up in a police safe house, there was always the possibility that he would find her. She didn't want to give him the opportunity to pick her off while she was asleep, maybe snipe her through a window.

That said, Emily was fully aware that even if she was fully awake, someone could do that. He could've done it no matter what state she was in. Plus, all things considered, he probably wouldn't do that while she was out in the open, in a very public, very well-lit hospital.

At the very least, Emily hoped that he wouldn't do that, that he wouldn't become more desperate now that he probably knew that Emily was in police protection.

All in all, she wondered if she would be able to get a little bit of sleep here in the hospital, particularly knowing that until the police took her somewhere, she didn't have anywhere else to go. But all the same, she didn't have the ability to fall asleep right now. She was too darn excited.

Ollie was alive. Ollie was going to make it. Emily hadn't done anything to destroy that family. It all worked out, and Mary was going to be able to hold onto her husband for a while longer.

It couldn't have happened more beautifully. Of everything that had happened, she was grateful that this one thing had worked out perfectly. Nobody else had to suffer like she did.

She was so happy that he was going to pull through, and she really wanted to see him and thank him for saving her life and almost risking giving his own. Unfortunately, rules were rules—strange thing to say after everything that had happened—and the hospital wasn't going to let any random person in to visit. So she would have to wait until he got a little healthier and his visitation rights reopened.

For this couple, though, Emily was willing to wait as long as she had to. And she felt she couldn't sleep a wink until it was time.

Looking up, Emily turned her attention to the television screen again. The news report had ended, and in its place, the channel had switched to a morning cooking show. Something not quite as aggressive as the reality television that she had grown accustomed to hearing about. This was more of a relaxing show, one where people seemed to have calm, rational discussions about food.

Emily was watching it as if she were seeing something like this for the very first time in her entire life. She had seen cooking shows in the past and certainly was aware of the stereotype of them. But this was something different.

Almost twelve hours ago, the photo had been slipped under her door telling her that her boyfriend was cheating on her. About six hours ago, she was traipsing through some dark forest out in the farmlands, running for her life. Everything had been falling apart in her life then. Everything was going to be destroyed. She'd felt like she didn't have anything left. It was weird to think that out of that state, she was able to get to a place where simple things like cooking shows still existed on television, and people were able to smile at each other and speak to each other like civilized human beings.

If things had turned out differently, Emily realized, she would've never seen two smiling people on a television set again. Her innards would be lying on the forest floor somewhere. She would have just been another dead victim of Daniel's.

If Daniel had his way. If Daniel were allowed to call the shots for—

Emily stopped. And stared off into space.

She only just realized it.

"Coffee?"

Emily shook herself out of her stupor and turned to the source of the request. Somehow, looking out into the middle of nowhere, she had barely noticed that the detective had showed up beside her again, holding two cups of coffee, offering one to Emily.

"Please," Emily said, reaching out with a smile and a nod. She happily took the coffee and drank it. Amazingly, it was still hot.

"I suppose you were under the impression that I was about to serve you cold, or at least terrible, coffee," said the detective, seemingly knowing what was running through Emily's mind. "Well, I hate to break it to you, but just because I'm a cop doesn't mean we're at the police station at the moment. You're drinking hospital coffee, which means it'll probably be pretty good."

Emily laughed before taking another sip of her coffee. It felt good to laugh again.

"See, that's the first step," she said in between sips of her own coffee. "Being able to look at the world again and enjoy it. It's what they want people who've been through your kind of traumatic situation to start doing. I regret to say that they haven't given quite a lot of information on exactly how you're supposed to do that, or how you're even expected to do that. Frankly, it's always disappointing me that they leave that aspect to the victims to figure out."

"Thank you," replied Emily. She didn't really know what to say at this time. It was odd to be treated so nicely, so politely. It almost felt alien after nearly being killed so many times tonight.

"Do you ever get tired of dealing with these sorts of cases? I mean, I honestly don't know how many of these cases you've had to handle. Maybe this is the first one? But maybe you've heard of other cases."

"What do you mean?" asked Detective Cole.

"I mean these guys who, for whatever reason, can't seem to take rejection. And they fall apart at the first sign of a strong woman. I don't know why the stereotype exists. Because if it does, there must be at least some instances of truth to support it, right?"

"I can assure you that as a middle-aged female detective in authority over an entire precinct of males, I have definitely encountered men who can't get over the idea of a strong woman."

"But then, why? I mean, why does it keep happening?"

"That's something you'll have to discuss with a philosopher, or possibly some sort of historical researcher into power dynamics, because at the end the day, what I've learned as a detective, as a woman, as . . . well, anything . . . is that I get angry. And I don't like having to deal with jerks or awful bosses or terrible news coming in from around the world. And for whatever reason, I don't decide to pick up a gun and kill someone over it. So maybe I have the opportunity to just lose it and let everything in my life fall apart, but I choose not to take it. And maybe it's a little bit of conservative thinking, and maybe it's not what you want to hear, but at the end of the day, even if there is some sort of fundamental truth to the differences between men and women, I have to believe that a man like Daniel Powers is given the opportunity to decide to stop doing the horrible things he does, and he chooses to fail instead. Because it's easy . . . because it's comfortable.

"Sorry for rambling. What brought this on?"

"Well, I just had a realization. Something that I wish I had brought up earlier, except I didn't think about it then."

"What is it?"

"I'm not so certain anymore that Daniel knows where I live."

"What do you mean?"

"He claimed to have left the photo under my door, right?"

"Yes."

"How could he do that and then race to Legal to beat me to the bar where he found me? And why would he go there? Did he know my boyfriend was there? How would he know?"

The detective set down her coffee and rested her hand against her knees. "All fair points, but the note he left for you included a photograph of your boyfriend with his lover, out on the street. Perhaps he was following him for some time as well. Perhaps, when he slid that photo under your door, he already knew where to track your boyfriend. And then he raced to follow him."

"Maybe. Still, it's hard to imagine him following Jeremy. After all, why didn't he kill him anytime sooner? Why now?"

"Perhaps to talk to you? To make you feel that he could get to you any time. Being able to get close to women and keep close to women whom he wanted to harass appears to be his main way of doing it, as I've just learned."

"What do you mean? What did you just learn?"

The detective sat up straight again and released a heavy sigh. "Ever since we put out that warrant, we've had officers around town trying to find any and all information about him, including previous residences. Using facial recognition software and that photo of him and his driver's license image that the news likes to bandy about, we were able to identify one of his earlier residences. Apparently, he lived across the hall from his first victim."

"Oh, my God," Emily whispered.

"I came back here to ask you if you were absolutely certain whether you'd seen him before."

29

It was a very reasonable thing to ask, Emily realized. But it didn't do anything to help alleviate her concerns.

She thought she understood it all. She thought that it made perfect sense that Daniel Powers had been stalking her for many weeks, if not months, or any length of time. Otherwise, why would he be putting so much effort into her? Why would he have this strong an obsession?

But talking it over with Detective Cole caused all the holes to start revealing themselves.

After all was said and done, how did Emily actually know that Daniel was the one who'd slipped that note underneath her door? Emily knew the answer to that one—it was because Daniel told her so himself. And she simply took him at his word. Why wouldn't she? What kind of person would say something crazy like that?

But that was really the thing about it, wasn't it? A crazy person would say something like that. A crazy person would take responsibility for a crime he'd never committed. And how else could she describe a man like Daniel Powers?

Somebody who put in every effort to seem as insane as possible.

Which meant that, for whatever reason, Daniel was obsessing over Emily, but why, exactly? Emily couldn't figure it out at first. But thankfully, that was what Detective Cole was for.

She was a remarkable woman. On the one hand, very professional and very adept at putting the pieces together, easily able to make smart and strong determinations about how to catch a perpetrator. About what was the next thing to do that would be the best choice. On the other hand, she never allowed her professionalism to overwhelm her life. She seemed empathetic. Calm, collected, but also very caring and open-minded.

Case in point, Detective Cole revealed to Emily that at one time in her career, long before becoming a detective, she'd moved up through the ranks of the police department in various fields. As a patrolman, as an officer on foot. But also, notably, as a sketch artist. Apparently, not only was she good at drawing faces, but she was also pretty skilled at getting people to talk about their experiences. Getting them to think about it, getting them to open up and concentrate carefully without being overwhelmed by dark emotions.

Emily realized that people who were spoken to calmly and sympathized with tended to be able to think about a situation without being scared of it. And therefore, they looked at it more carefully. They remembered it better.

Emily put her feet up on the hospital waiting room seat and enjoyed listening to the soothing sound of Detective Cole's voice as they just talked amicably. The detective made her feel that she was in safe hands with the police department. All the while, Detective Cole held onto her tablet and with an electronic stylus sketched an accurate depiction of what Daniel Powers looked like from Emily's words.

At first, when the detective suggested this, Emily wondered whether it would be helpful. After all, the news report clearly proved that they had an image of Daniel Powers. They already knew what he looked like. But Detective Cole revealed that she already knew about the photo and that the photo was easily about seven years old. People changed over that amount of time, and being able to provide the police with more information about newly developed wrinkles and bags under his eyes, or possibly a receding hairline, could prove very useful in ensuring that the police didn't question their own eyes when they looked for the man out on the street.

And Emily found that she could help in this way. Detective Cole's technique of speaking almost therapeutically worked. Emily was able to look back on the evening—the taunting, the stalking, the gunshots, the harassment—and she was able to look at it in a way that Emily had gone through great difficulties and gained great strength. She slowly became a better person for it.

She was able to face the night. She felt like she could actually face a horrible man like Daniel.

It made it easier for her to look back on this crazed lunatic following her up and down the highway, yelling obscene things at her. She was able to think about him a little more clearly, think about just how much weight was in his cheeks, how tired his eyes looked.

Emily was able to think about how crazy he really acted, how determined he was to make everything about himself.

Yes, Emily realized. A man like that would definitely take the credit for a crime he never committed if he honestly believed it made him sound preferable in his mind.

Which, Emily realized, suggested that maybe Daniel Powers never actually knew her. Maybe he really did stumble upon her in that bar. He could have heard her tell Jeremy that the photo had been slipped under the door, but she couldn't remember whether she had actually said that or not. She probably had.

Maybe that was just his method of operation. After all, Detective Cole had revealed that the bar in Legal was the location where he'd met his third victim. Sure, he'd followed the woman there, but maybe he realized the potential of finding women in such an out-of-the-way bar, so he just hung around, waiting to find somebody new.

Until he found Emily.

Emily wasn't sure if that made him more or less dangerous. On the one hand, he obviously wasn't trying to track her, at first at least, if any of this was true. But on the other hand, did that mean that he just picked out any woman at random? As long as they maybe lived across from him, or came within sight of him, or barely talked to him?

If anything, it made him sound like some wild animal, lashing out randomly.

No, Emily thought. *Not a wild animal.* Even the wild animals in the forest tonight never attacked her because they knew how to act rationally for their food. They didn't attack for no reason. Daniel Powers was more like a crazed, rabid animal.

One that she knew deserved to be put down.

Detective Cole turned her tablet to Emily, offering her a view of the screen. "Do you think he looked something like this?"

Emily almost snapped back into attention. Listening to the detective's maternal voice, feeling empathized with and cared for, made her feel very welcome, very secure. Emily almost didn't realize that in the entire time she'd been sitting there with the detective, she had finished her sketch. Emily didn't feel interrogated at all. In fact, if anything, she almost felt better.

She looked down at the tablet. There, in all his disgusting glory, was the face of her attacker. It was almost like the one on the news reports, but there was a slight difference about it, a kind of unkemptness that felt like it added a bit of character.

"Yeah," Emily said. "Yeah, that's him."

The detective looked at her work again. "That's good. I'll send this out to the precinct and tell them to update their files. If we can get this out soon enough, then maybe there's a better chance some patrolman won't pass him by. Thank you for all your help." She got up and turned toward the door.

Emily panicked. "Wait, you're leaving?"

"Yes, I should join in the search too."

"But what about me? I still don't have a place to stay . . ."

"We have officers outside. And I think they finally finished looking through Powers's apartment, so I need to get back to seeing if we got any results from that."

"But those officers outside, they're gonna be looking around all over the place, and he'll just come sneak by them and . . ." Emily didn't know how to finish her statement. She didn't know how to express to the detective that, in all likelihood, Daniel could find a way to get past any of these cops and get to her as she was alone in the hospital waiting room. She didn't know how to explain that even without her help, he probably should've been caught by now.

She didn't know how else to say that she didn't really trust the police officers. She trusted Detective Cole.

Fortunately, the detective smiled at her. She didn't have to.

"I suppose," the detective said, rolling her eyes, "I could keep in touch with everybody from here remotely. It's not like it's the end of the world if I'm not the one to catch him."

"Thank you," said Emily, resting back in her seat. For a moment there, she felt like she was back on that highway.

30

E mily watched as Detective Cole tapped away on her tablet, presumably keeping in touch with the officers she had been working with while trying to track down Daniel Powers. Emily was hoping that the detective didn't think she was wasting her time on Emily's account. She didn't want to gain a negative reputation with the only officer who made her feel like she was safe at the moment. She didn't want to feel as if this woman looked down on her.

That, and obviously, she also didn't want Detective Cole to be taken away from her job of tracking down this guy. She didn't like the idea that maybe, just maybe, she was actually causing the detective to do a poor job by not being closer to her resources.

But if she told the detective to go, she would be alone again. Just as alone as she had been in the deep, dark forest. Along that infinite, aggravating highway. All in the darkness, surrounded by the cold wind, the dirty disgusting water . . . and the blood.

She didn't want to think about the blood anymore. It was too excruciating.

Emily wanted to be free of it, but the only way she could feel as if she could have some kind of freedom from that was whenever she was around other people. Ollie was off in a hospital room, and Mary was staying by his side. Detective Cole was good enough to keep her company now, but strictly speaking, Emily knew it wasn't her job.

Was this her life now? she wondered. Was she always going to be scared? Constantly looking over her shoulder, holding onto people, making sure she was never alone again. Locking every door, shutting every window, not that doing so had kept Daniel out of Ollie and Mary's house.

Honestly, that was the way she had been living ever since she had become an adult, anyway. It wasn't like she hadn't taken basic safety precautions as a woman most of her adult life. But now, it became painfully distressing how necessary it was, how close she had gotten, so many times this evening, to being killed.

She wondered if it was worth it to live this way, to effectively become a burden on everybody around her. Would Detective Cole become her new best friend?

If they couldn't find Daniel, would she live in a police safe house for the rest of her life? Or would that be a drain on municipal resources, and she would eventually have to pay rent for that as well?

And now that she thought about it, how in the world would she be able to pay rent? Would she have to go back to her waitressing job? It wouldn't take Daniel long to find her there, ruin everything, maybe kill her, maybe kill everybody around her. Of course, she could probably go back to her job sitting at a computer, typing away at useless nonsense for incompetent morons with deep pockets and poor self-editing skills. She wasn't really sure if that, perhaps, was a worse fate than death.

She wasn't sure what her life would look like from now

on. And unfortunately, in their current state, the police didn't either. They were too busy looking for a perpetrator and probably investigating a few dead bodies and an apartment in the process. She wondered when would be the right time to ask Detective Cole if her room was ready. How long would she have to wait before it wouldn't sound like a demand or an unreasonable request? How long before she would make herself a burden on the detective even more than she already had?

This was what she had become, Emily thought. She had become a waste on people's lives.

Detective Cole suddenly straightened up. Apparently, somebody was approaching Emily from behind, and the detective noticed long before Emily did. One more reason to apologize to Detective Cole for making her work overtime.

Emily turned around. It was Dr. Styles from earlier.

"Hello," he said to Emily. "You're the Rosses' friend, aren't you?"

"I guess. I mean, yeah. Why?"

"I just thought you should know that Mrs. Ross said that you're welcome to come up to his new room if you're still here."

"New room?"

"Mr. Ross has been in recovery, but we decided that his body was still pretty weak after the gunshot. So we'd like to keep him overnight for observation. No reason to keep him the ER, so we've moved him to a regular hospital room. He's resting there, and he's probably sleeping, but he is now open to other visitors, and it seems his wife has specifically requested that you be welcomed to see him."

For the life of her, Emily couldn't understand why. She felt as if some mistake had been made, and she really shouldn't be allowed to see anybody.

All the same, she was starting to feel restless. She got up

and couldn't help but notice out of the corner of her eye, somebody was moving with her.

She turned rapidly, startled at the moving body before realizing that it was Detective Cole, who simply rose to accompany her to Ollie's room.

Emily dropped her face down into her hand. For a moment, she honestly believed that maybe it was Daniel who suddenly showed up next to her. She had forgotten that the detective was there the entire time.

Now she was seeing things. *Just wonderful*, she thought.

All the same, it was time to take a walk. The doctor led the way as Emily and Detective Cole followed.

When they walked through the door, there were other hospital staff there, doing their jobs, milling about. Emily's chest was filled with cold every time she realized there were more people. Her eyes kept shifting around, trying to spot a face. She quickly realized that she was suffering from paranoia, and she was terrified that at any moment, someone was going to come and attack her. But just because she was aware of it didn't mean that she was able to brush it off.

This was a very real terror, and she felt that it wasn't over yet.

Whenever she rounded a corner, she slowed down, scared to see who was on the other side of it. Eventually, she felt a hand placed gently on her back and wondered if somebody had leapt out from behind until she looked around and saw it was Detective Cole, gently trying to prod her along, getting her to keep moving with confidence.

Emily smiled but didn't want to tell the detective what she was thinking. This was not the time to be touching her. This was not the time to surprise her. Dammit, she was ready to turn around and slash her face off.

Finally, they got up to the floor, and Mary practically leapt up and put her arms around Emily. Emily couldn't imagine why. Whether she was grateful to her for something or just worried about her, Emily felt that it was undeserved. She felt like she would fall apart at any moment.

And then she rounded the doorway and looked in the hospital room. There, in a gown, with an IV inserted into his arm, lay Ollie, looking helpless and weak. Looking like he could go at any moment.

Emily had to assume that Mary had brought her up here to be able to see him, to see that he was all right. She tried to smile gratefully but didn't let on what she was really thinking, that it really had the opposite effect. When she looked down at Ollie, all she could see was the fact that he was here because of her, that if they had never met her and, instead, she had simply died somewhere out alone in that forest, then Mary and Ollie would be able to continue living out their lives without any surprises.

But this? This suffering, this needless pain. This was all she had left to offer to anybody.

Emily stood silently as Mary offered some platitudes—Emily felt all of them were empty and weak—before Mary said that she was going to sleep in this room and needed to get some rest.

Emily got the hint and politely said goodbye and stepped out of the room.

Outside, Detective Cole waited politely. "Sounds like they were really worried about you."

"Worried about me?" said Emily, confused. "Why?"

"They put quite a lot of effort into making sure that you were all right. And I guess they could've blamed you for this, but they wanted you to get closer to see Ollie, just to remind you that they were very welcoming to you. That they still want you nearby. They obviously could've asked you to leave or not bothered with you anymore at all."

"Maybe they should have."

"I'm not about to go around calling myself a psychiatrist or anything like that. But I guess the only amateur advice I can offer is, at a certain point, the only one who can really make the decision as to whether that's true or not is you. But for what it's worth, from the outside, everyone seems to disagree with you. Everyone seems to be glad that you're okay. And it might be good to remember that."

Emily started thinking about what the detective said to her and whether it was actually true.

But she barely got a chance to think about it because a gunshot rang out from the floor below.

31

For a moment, Emily wondered if maybe she was hearing things or maybe there was some piece of technology in the hospital environment that would've simulated the sound of a gunshot, and it wasn't what it obviously, most certainly was.

But then again, she had already been through this earlier that evening.

She looked over at Detective Cole and saw the determination in her face, the slight hint of fear in the pupils of her eyes. That was the only reinforcement she needed.

If the professional detective was concerned that it was something more than just ambient noise, then Emily knew that there was good reason to be concerned. This wasn't her imagination. This wasn't hospital mechanisms. This was the real thing.

Somebody had fired a gun on the floor below.

She looked down the hallway and saw numerous hospital staff either running or walking with intent toward various emergency exits.

"It's Daniel," Emily said, "isn't it?"

"If it is," said Detective Cole, pulling out her own gun, "then I must be working with some of the stupidest people on the police force in the history of the planet. Because either they allowed themselves to get killed or allowed a single assailant to sneak by them, or they were so far away from the hospital that they weren't able to actually do anything by virtue of not even being here."

"Didn't you send them all off into the city to search for Daniel?"

"It's not like we only have six guys. Of course we have enough people to guard the outside of the hospital. What the hell were they doing that they just let anybody in?"

Both the detective and Emily proceeded down the hallway in the direction of the evacuating orderlies. Suddenly, a lot of the orderlies that she had seen running in one direction were now running in the opposite direction. In fact, Emily watched as one of them turned and entered their hallway.

"Would you come on?" Cole said to the man, grabbing him by the shoulders. "You! What's going on? Why haven't you evacuated?"

The orderly looked like he was probably still in med school, barely a kid. He also looked like he was about to have a nervous breakdown.

"All the doors are locked," he said, trying not to cry, his voice quavering. "I don't know what happened, but somebody activated the biohazard protocols. The whole building is shut tight, and nothing can get in or out."

"Can't you turn that off?"

"That's not so easy. Even if you skip safety checks and hurry things along, it still won't open for a good, I don't know, twenty minutes?"

"Well, shit," Detective Cole spat.

Emily could see that the woman was frustrated, clearly in a bind. She was in a situation with a gunman downstairs, and she couldn't get any backup. She was on her own, and she had a building full of potential victims.

She figured that was why the detective must've made her next choice. What she must've felt was probably the dumbest decision of her career.

"Get to a safe room," she told the orderly as she ran off down the hallway toward the commotion. "Lock the door behind you. And don't open it unless you know who it is." In a flash, the detective was gone around the corner.

Emily couldn't believe it. In the haste of the panic of the situation, Detective Cole had completely forgotten about Emily. She'd left her alone.

Emily imagined that, in any other situation, the detective would've probably hurried her along to police custody or at least kept her with her while keeping her as far away from the floor with a gunman as possible. Instead, she sprang into action and put Emily into the back of her mind.

Emily turned on her heel and ran for the emergency exit.

Emily also considered the possibility that maybe this was a premeditated decision on Detective Cole's part. After all, she wasn't exactly left with a lot of options herself. She didn't have any backup, and she didn't have any reason to think that the gunman was going to stop firing or hurting people. She was the only person who was able to take care of the situation. Maybe, under these extreme circumstances, Emily figured that all other people, all other matters, would be brushed aside.

Emily would be brushed aside. This early in the morning, and Daniel was still deciding what her value was.

When she reached the emergency exit, Emily looked down the concrete stairwell and raced to the floor below. She was certain that was the floor where Daniel was going to be, as it was the ER floor.

Daniel, the electronics engineering tech wizard who was able to shut down cell phone and internet services across an entire region and provide himself with the one phone that wasn't affected. Daniel, who knew how to shut down the power to a house but still leave a single power source available so that he could power a buzz saw to get in through a door. And if there was one person she could count on to be able to trigger a safety system into locking all the doors by falsifying a biohazard emergency, it would be him.

He controlled everything. He loved feeling in control. He loved being on top of his world, on top of women.

Emily got to the emergency door in the stairwell that led to the ER floor, and she stopped. Because that was the case, wasn't it? He really did know how to control women. He really did love it. It was what made him tick.

That's the key, Emily realized.

Launching onto the floor, she didn't know the sections of the hospital. But by this point, she figured it wouldn't really be hard to figure out where Daniel was.

Just look for the source of panic.

She ran down one hallway and quickly turned left around a corner. She ran down that hallway and saw signs indicating that ER operations were to the right. She turned right and ran through some doors. There was nobody there.

That's a good sign, she thought. It meant that everybody had evacuated.

Everybody except one.

By the time she got farther down the hallway, she could hear him screaming.

"Where the fuck is the bitch?" his unmistakable voice cried out. "I want the bitch. I want Emily. I'm going to fucking shoot everybody unless I get Emily!"

By the time he finished ranting, Emily had finally come upon him. He was standing just outside the rehabilitation room doors, grabbing a very scared-looking young nurse, his revolver pointed at her temple. He looked wild, manic, desperate.

He looked very honest, somehow, Emily thought.

"Let her go!" Emily shouted.

Daniel flipped around, still holding onto his hostage.

She looked like she was crying, like she was never going to see her family again. Like everything was falling apart for her. Like she was just going to be his next victim now.

"Okay," he said, still pointing his gun at the nurse's head. "Babe, just come on over here, and we can leave."

Emily knew what to do. "Do you actually need a hostage?"

Daniel froze. He looked at the woman he was holding, then looked back toward Emily. "What?" he said suddenly.

"I thought you were a big man. I thought you could handle yourself. Where the fuck is the guy who could laugh at me while I was up in a tree? Ha-ha-ha! Where the fuck is that guy, huh?"

Emily watched as the look on Daniel's face drained of all color. He was embarrassed. He was hurting.

She was loving it.

"Where is the big man with the pickup lines at the bar? What, you need a girl to protect you? You need to hide behind your mommy's skirt? Have her pat you on your head, suckle you with some milk from her titties? Just a big old puss, that's what you are!"

"Fuck you."

"Come on. I've got your balls right here. Fucking loser. I would never fucking sleep with you."

"Fuck you!"

Daniel threw his hostage to the side. He apparently

couldn't care less about her anymore. He was clearly angry that he was being spoken to in this way. By another woman. By Emily.

The woman who had defeated him all night long.

He yelled as he charged toward Emily.

32

E mily's jaw dropped. Here Daniel was, a man with a gun who could easily shoot her.

And he was charging right at her.

Emily flinched when she heard gunshots. She thought that, somehow, she'd missed seeing him lift his gun and didn't notice him killing her.

But after her body calmed down and the shock wore off, she realized that nothing had touched her, and she was fine.

Daniel, on the other hand, fell forward and collapsed in a heap on the floor.

Behind him, Detective Cole was holding her recently fired Glock. She had put a pair of bullets in Daniel Powers's back.

Emily didn't trust it, though. She had to be certain. She ran up to Daniel's body and looked down. There was no breathing, no movement. He wasn't going for his gun. He wasn't doing anything at all except lying there. Dead.

Emily felt no sympathy. In fact, the only thought going through her head was that Daniel had died in the way he would've hated the most. He had been brought down by a woman. Two, depending on how one looked at it.

She had long ago abandoned feeling bad about turning into this kind of person.

Later, Emily sat in the waiting room, in the same seat that she had spent almost the entire evening. Only this time, the medics had managed to shut down the security protocols and get the doors open. The room was now filled with police officers.

Emily was certain that they were here to deal with Daniel's corpse, but she also started wondering if any of them were going to arrest her.

After all, she had interfered with a police investigation by running off and confronting the gunman herself, putting herself in danger. Emily wondered if there was some sort of bylaw for that as well.

Sure enough, Detective Cole approached her in time. "You know what I'm supposed to say to you," the detective said, smiling and nodding. "But I'm not going to. For three reasons. You know why?"

"Why?"

"Well, one, you would have to be really stupid to not already know how incredibly reckless that was. Two, if your story of what happened to you this evening is any indication, I figured you'd probably been through enough. And three, well . . . I imagine that my superiors wouldn't be very happy with me if they knew that the reason that man was here in the first place was that I left a woman unsupervised and unprotected while I went off to find him. So there's enough stupid to go around. I guess what I'm trying to say is I can keep a secret if you can."

"Yeah, that's fair. But do you wanna know what I was thinking?"

"What's that?"

"I feel completely confident that if I hadn't gotten there,

you probably would've beaten me to him. And well, you know what to do with a gun."

"Still pretty irresponsible, though. After all, it's not like any of us are superheroes."

Emily nodded. She knew she had been inches away from death in that situation. But that said, she already knew that she had been in many dangerous and deadly situations the entire evening. By this point, she had lost the will to feel panicked about anything.

That, and she had to get used to the idea that her assailant was dead.

It was maybe the dozenth time that she thought it was all over. But it was the first time that it felt like it was actually true.

The detective sat down next to her and pretty much ran through what was on her mind. "I guess one of the good things about something like this happening in the hospital is that the medical report can come pretty quickly. There are over a dozen doctors here who were able to confirm that the bullets went straight into the man's heart. He died instantly. They still did the medically ethical thing and checked whether they needed to pronounce him dead or try to revive him." She shrugged. "But you know. Doctors."

Emily was glad they hadn't attempted to revive him.

"Aside from that, now that the power has been restored to a lot of areas north of the city, I'm getting reports from several sheriffs' departments about what's been going on up there. I guess he must've figured that by now, they found the bodies of your ex-boyfriend and his lover. We filled them in on what you told us. We also sent them over to the Ross estate. They'll be contacting Mrs. Ross to get permission to investigate the area.

"Also, they sent some people up to Legal. They'll be taking care of your car. And Miss Flint's car. And I think they logged a report of the bartender being punched that night. But based on what I've heard, they're just going to throw it into the pile of all the other reports they heard about violence being conducted in that bar. Apparently, it's a recurring thing up there. Don't know if you wanted to know."

Emily froze for a moment. It sounded almost as if Detective Cole not only knew about her conduct but was willing to sweep it under the rug. Emily couldn't imagine why, except for with everything that had happened to her, maybe a misdemeanor wasn't worth the hassle. Or maybe it was her weird, unusual way of showing gratitude for helping take down a horrible perpetrator.

Like she said, she could keep a secret.

"What about Daniel?" Emily asked. "I don't mean the body. I don't know what I mean. Maybe the investigation, or—"

"We finished searching his apartment. From what I can tell you, it was a pretty sad sight. There's very little in there that anybody, as he guessed, any woman, would want to see in a man's private home. It was mostly stacks of papers, things he was too lazy to throw out. Electronics, computers, TV screens. And porn. Lots and lots of porn. Really disturbing stuff.

"Which, apparently, was the name of the game when it came to investigating this guy's stuff. Oh, his paper notes were just random things he wrote down. Various measurements, notes about getting groceries, quick things, stuff like that. The real creepy stuff was when we finally got into his computer files. That's when we realized that he effectively kept two different hard drives. One was work related and had a lot of electronic data on it perfectly expected for an electronic engineer like him.

"The other computer hard drive was where he lived out his life. It was basically a long, sad electronic journal of all his wishes and dreams. I was going to have a couple of officers read it to try to find any evidence that might help us track him down, see about tracking his movements. Not much point to it now, of course, except maybe as a psychological profile investigation for university or law students. But from what I'm told, based on the initial look at it, it was an extremely long diatribe, more like him putting freeform thoughts onto the keyboard.

"And it was him just hating women. Hating everything about women's bodies, women's voices, women's actions, women's opinions. It was like there were three groups in the world. There was himself, then all the various men in the world, which he seemed to acknowledge as a collection of unique individuals, all of them, obviously, less impressive than himself. And then, women were just this . . . one thing. One concept. And he was angry at them, and he hated them. And he lived out rape fantasies and sex fantasies and domination fantasies on them in his words."

Emily shivered.

"At a certain point, the journal entries almost stopped. Almost. It's not that he stopped writing entirely, but it stopped being wish fulfilment. It stopped being multiple pages long. No. After that, it just became a normal journal. Short details. Things he did, described in a few words or sentences. Instructions on drinking more water or getting more exercise. And explaining the condition of the other women's bodies and what he had to do to dispose of them."

Emily's eyes widened. "He actually wrote it all down?"

Detective Cole nodded. "That was probably the worst part of it all. Not the hatred or the grotesqueness of the murderous words, but the fact that this change in his writing style came about at approximately the time when we estimate those poor women died. He actually lived out his fantasies, and it was like a release for him. Like he had this incredible tension in his soul that he finally got to let go of, and he was cleansed. He actually became . . . ugh, it's just sick thinking about it, but he became something similar to normal. Or at least as normal as possible."

"He was not normal," Emily insisted.

"No, you're right, he wasn't. This is usually the hardest part of the job, especially dealing with this sort of psychotic person. The realization of uncomfortable and hard realities. What we're dealing with here was a guy who, if he were actually allowed to do anything he wanted with women . . . then he probably would've just psychologically and chemically leveled out and would seem like an ordinary person any other time he was out and about."

"Or he'd go even more psycho," Emily put in.

"Maybe. But that's what these serial killers all live for. That's what they believe. They sincerely believe that they have this aggravating itch, like a phantom limb that tells them something is wrong. And if they just give themselves permission to scratch it, they'll actually get to finally be at peace. Then they blame everybody else around them for not letting them be at peace. That's the real horror of these situations. They think of themselves as victims, fighting against an extremely oppressive, offensive attacker."

"I don't care how he felt, honestly," Emily declared. "He was never the victim."

"No, he wasn't," the detective said. "And your standing up to him like you did, well . . . you proved him wrong. You challenged him and made him stop and debate his actions, his thoughts, his words, like an adult. You showed him that he might be wrong. He could have shot you, but you confused him, and in doing so, he couldn't function and reverted to charging at you. It destroyed him."

After a long silence, Detective Cole stood up. "I'm not really sure what I get out of saying this to you. I think I just needed to be able to hear it out loud. Or maybe I'm just grateful to be able to thank you for helping in your own way. But I wanted you to know that you should never put yourself in that kind of danger again. You can take it from my own personal experience. It's obvious why these people do what they do. In a sense, it's almost obvious how to stop it, how to prevent it from happening again. And yet, every generation, there's always some new asshole who thinks he's the center of the world. And I usually have to deal with him. So for once . . . I guess I just want to say thank you for helping."

Detective Cole passed along her business card, probably as a formality or just in case Emily needed her help again. And then she turned and walked off to her colleagues.

Emily stared at the card with the phone number on it. She didn't know what in the world she would be using it for. She didn't want to do this on a regular basis. She hadn't wanted to help the police deal with this maniac, let alone another one. She didn't want any of this. She didn't want to be responsible for it.

She almost felt like she would never sleep again.

33

The subject of a safe house for Emily never came up again. And she never expected it to. After all, she certainly didn't need it anymore. Everyone kept telling her that her assailant was dead. She was hoping that eventually it would sink in and feel like it was true.

Instead, after helping fill out several reports and answering considerably more questions, a police officer offered her a ride back to her apartment. She happily took it. She finally started to feel as if she was ready to nod off.

She sat in the back of the car, separated from the driver and his partner by a plastic sheet with metal wiring within. The doors were also padded and locked so that anybody inside wouldn't be able to open them. The driver and his partner kept talking to her, politely, as if simply having a mild and calm conversation, like a taxi driver. Emily vaguely remembered paying attention and responding with simple words. Though, for the life of her, she couldn't remember what any of the conversations were. It all seemed too surreal. She spent the entire evening assuming that if she found herself in a police car, it would be to get dragged off to prison.

Now she had the assurance that it wasn't going to happen and that she wouldn't have to deal with any more police involvement in her life again.

When they arrived at her apartment building, the officers gave her their business cards as well, just in case she needed to call them for assistance.

She slipped the cards into her pocket next to the business card she already had from Detective Cole. She wondered if this was some sort of standard-issue formality that officers of the law engaged in to ensure that their butts were covered, providing citizens with an assurance that if they ever needed help, they could always reach out to the police. She wondered how many people ever took them up on this offer. For her part, she would throw those business cards into the trash the moment she got a chance.

After politely waving to the officers as they drove out of her neighborhood, she reached into the pocket of her borrowed sweatpants, pulled out her building keys, entered, and proceeded up to her apartment.

Her and Jeremy's apartment.

Walking in, everything was left the way she remembered it from yesterday afternoon. A little bit of food had been left to get hard, cold, and stale on the kitchen counter. There was still a mess on the bed and from the closet when she had searched through Jeremy's things.

Emily realized that if she cleaned them up and put them back where they were, they would just stay there. All of Jeremy's things were just things now. He was never going to come back for them.

And curiously enough, Emily couldn't care less.

It was the first point when she started to notice it. She couldn't be bothered with the conversations of the police officers in the car. She couldn't be bothered with Jeremy's things.

She figured the appropriate thing would be to contact

Jeremy's parents and let them know what had happened. Maybe they could take all of his things.

For the briefest of moments, she told herself she would call them after a long sleep, and then she wondered why that sounded perfectly reasonable to her. Wouldn't it have been better to contact them as quickly as possible and help them deal with the grief of losing their son?

But that would imply that she cared.

Emily thought about it for a moment. She was wondering how she was supposed to feel about all of this. It was barely twenty hours ago when somebody had slipped a note under her door, revealing her boyfriend's infidelity. She wondered if she should still feel enraged or betrayed. After that, she'd found his body. She was wondering if maybe she should be feeling disgusted or remorseful for hating him so much.

All in all, she didn't feel any of those things. She felt tired; she felt . . . almost bored.

If she had to say that she felt anything, it was relief that it was all behind her.

And if anything, that filled her with a sense of curiosity because it really didn't feel like her at all.

Suddenly, there was a knock at the door. Emily briefly wondered if Daniel had somehow risen from the grave and come after her again. Then she stopped to think that far more likely, the police had forgotten something.

She gingerly stepped over to the peephole and looked through. It was Nate Morrison, her next-door neighbor from across the hall. It was weird to think that he still existed. He seemed to be part of the life that had happened ages ago. She opened the door.

"Oh," he said as if he wasn't expecting the door to open. "Hi, you're here."

"Yeah?" she replied.

"No, I mean, yes, I guess you would be here. I was just

surprised, that's all. I was knocking on your door last night. I was worried that maybe something happened."

"What do you mean?"

There was an awkward silence.

Nate couldn't seem to look into her eyes; then he finally spoke up. "Okay, so look, I noticed that whenever you are going off to work at night, or something like that, there's, like . . . some other woman shows up and comes into your place. I don't know what's going on, but it started looking suspicious, and the more I thought about it, the more the guy you live with really never seems to bring it up and never seems to have the two of you here at the same time, so I thought that . . . maybe something was going on. Something that wasn't, you know, right."

Oh, my God, Emily thought. She already knew exactly where this was going. And she didn't want it to.

"So I thought," Nate continued, "that if I . . . By any chance, did you see a note under your door last night?"

"You left that note underneath my door?"

"Yeah, but I didn't hear anything after that, so I was wondering if he didn't come back last night—"

"Why didn't you just tell me?" She frowned at him, wondering why he'd really done it.

"Well, nobody likes to get cheated on or . . ."

Emily could see it in his eyes. He was embarrassed for her.

She sighed. "It's fine. Look, I need to go. It's been a long night."

He looked back up at her, apparently not ready to let her go. "Um, did you get into a fight? I . . ." He trailed off as he took in the scratches all over her face. This wasn't going the way he'd planned it to go, she could tell.

She nodded. "You could say that."

"Do you need me to kick his ass?" he asked.

Emily nearly snorted at the thought. "No, but thank you all the same," she tried to say as politely as possible but not having the heart for it. "I appreciate the offer. Thank you, really."

Nate smiled. "No problem. The offer, uh, still stands, you know? You've always really been great as my neighbor. And hey, if you ever want to discuss things, like, over coffee or a beer or something, maybe we could—"

"Maybe," she murmured, not really meaning it. Nate seemed like a nice guy, but after everything she'd just been through, she couldn't see herself getting involved with him or with anyone for a long, long time. "I need to go." She couldn't be bothered with being overly polite after the nightmare of the last twenty-four hours.

"Sure, sure," Nate said, nodding as he backed away from her door.

Emily closed the door and locked it before dragging herself to her room. She fell face first onto the bed and buried her face into her pillows. Now and forever, her lonely pillows.

Sometimes, it's just better not to feel anything, Emily thought.

And then she fell asleep immediately.

It was the best sleep she'd ever had in her life.

THANK YOU FOR READING

Did you enjoy reading *I Won't Let You Go?* Please consider leaving a review on Amazon. Your review will help other readers to discover the novel.

ABOUT THE AUTHOR

Cole Baxter loves writing psychological suspense thrillers. It's all about that last reveal that he loves shocking readers with.

He grew up in New York, where there was crime all around. He decided to turn that into something positive with his fiction.

His stories will have you reading through the night—they are very addictive!

ALSO BY COLE BAXTER

Inkubator Books Titles

The Perfect Suitor

The Betrayal

I Won't Let You Go

The Night Nurse

The Doppelganger

The Couple Next Door

I Will Find You

The Cole Baxter Box Set

Other Titles

Prime Suspect

What She Witnessed

Deadly Truth

Finding The Other Woman

Trust A Stranger

Follow You

Did He Do It

What Happened Last Night

Perfect Obsession

Going Insane

She's Missing

The Perfect Nanny

What She Forgot

Stolen Son

Before She's Gone

Made in the USA
Coppell, TX
08 March 2024

29883528R00152